THE MAN BELOW

THE MAN BELOW

KEVIN TUMLINSON

PROLOGUE

Run, run, don't be slow!
Never stop running from the man below!
–Anonymous, excerpted from *A South Texas Ghost Tale*

THERE HAD BEEN no light for nearly six days.

Or for fifty days.

By this point, the only reference for time that Clara had was the dim display of a computer monitor on the other side of the glass—a computer that may as well have been in another universe. And the time was a digital clock screensaver in 12-hour format, bouncing from corner to corner. No date. No indication of PM or AM. Seeing 12:00 could mean noon or it could mean midnight, she could never be certain.

It was Schrödinger's screensaver. *Maddening.*

She'd lost track of how many noons had passed—or how many midnights. She thought it was six, but it could have been more. It probably was more.

The door was locked. From the inside and the outside. She wasn't sure if that relieved or terrified her at the moment.

The darkness pressed in on her, squeezing her. She could feel it in her straining eyes, in her temples, in her *skin*.

You don't get used to darkness like this. The faint light of a computer monitor on the other side of six inches of lead-lined glass was not adequate for dispelling this kind of darkness.

Five miles below the surface.

Every door, in all five miles, locked.

You are in a room where no one will ever find you—no one that you *want* to find you.

No one could hear her screaming, and she'd given that up days ago. Or hours ago. Again, she wasn't sure.

She had food and water. Plenty. This was a military-grade bunker, after all. Or something like one—definitely military, definitely a big secret, buried out here in the mountains of New Mexico, five miles from a former experimental aircraft test site. Fifty miles from the nearest person who might, by some miracle, hear her scream for help.

Her only hope was the cell phone.

Before she'd run in here, before she'd managed to escape the man with the face tattoo—the *Comrade*—she'd sent a text message. It was her last text, before dropping the phone, letting it tumble into the grate, down into the flow of water, out to God knew where. It might be lost. But it might find its way out, into some place where there was sunshine and open air and, God willing, a cell phone signal.

It was a hope. The slimmest hope. She'd gambled everything on it, and she clung to it now, cringing in the darkness, sometimes squeezing her eyes shut to stop the damned clock from bouncing.

She wasn't an idiot. She was a scientist. She was a reasonable person and a rational thinker. She kept repeating these things like mantras, trying to convince herself that tossing the phone into the grate had been a strategy, not a mistake.

It was logical. It made sense. Even if it made no sense at all.

That grate led to a stream of flowing water. She'd heard it while she was hiding, keeping herself wedged between two large tanks, praying the Comrade didn't hear her breathing.

There was no signal in here. She had no way to reach the outside world. But she was a scientist—she knew how this technology worked. Text messaging had a better shot of getting through with a weak signal.

Of course, here, in the Pit, she had no signal at all. And no way out, with the Comrade chasing her, cutting her off from every exit.

Every exit except the grate—the tiny, narrow path that she'd never fit through in a million years. But her phone could. Her phone, with the drop-proof, shock-proof, *water* proof case. The floating case that had let her find it at the lake. The case that had kept it safe even that time she'd dropped it in a fountain. The case that she was counting on now to keep the phone safe, keep it afloat, straight through the drain and out into the world somewhere.

If it could be pushed out of the mountain, out into the open, it might reach some place that had a signal. And then it could send that last text.

That text could save her. It *had* to save her.

Because otherwise...

She whimpered, curled in on herself there in the darkness. It was her millionth whimper. It wouldn't be her last.

She didn't want to whimper, though. Didn't want to hear it, echoing from the stone walls of this room, with its racks of food and its lead-lined window into another room she'd never reach, and the door that had to be three-feet thick.

Three-feet of steel. Six inches of lead-lined glass. Five miles of stone and dirt above.

She was going to die here, if that text didn't go through. She would die here, alone in this darkness, with nothing but an aging computer monitor and an infuriating screensaver for company.

The man with the face tattoo—the *Comrade*—he was still out there, too.

So she was not entirely alone.

Instead of giving her comfort, this only made her guts clench worse, made the feeling in her chest tighten, made her want to vomit and scream at the same time.

Occasionally the Comrade tried to get in. Not as much as he had at first, not as loudly or frantically. But he was out there, and he kept coming back. Kept scraping that... that *thing* against the door.

Long. Metal. Jagged and sharp. Like a scythe, like the one tattooed on his face, but... not. Different. Less refined. More organic.

More monstrous.

It looked less like a weapon and more like some gruesome extension of the Comrade's arm. A dark, ragged, *thirsty* thing.

Something *hungry* for her.

Clara whimpered again, and curled in on herself, hugging her knees to her chest, praying for the first time since she was a teenager. Praying to a God she hadn't believed in, hadn't *wanted* to believe in, for more than a decade now.

But now, curled and cowering in the dark, she clung to God as her only hope.

Well... God... and a text message.

· · ·

THE PHONE WAS in a waterproof case, bought specifically because its owner had dropped and destroyed half a dozen previous models. The phone's owner was an active person—she put herself and her phone in a lot of precarious places. So it was inevitable that there were many phones before this one.

The phone was the latest—possibly the last—in a long line of devices that had met their fates with smashed screens, dropped from high places or run over by car tires, their electronics fried when they were accidentally put in microwave ovens, or shorted out when they were dropped into toilets. Or just plain left in the back seats of Ubers or in research libraries or at airports or restaurants or God only knew where else.

There had been many phones before this one.

The waterproof, impact-proof case had saved this phone, though, on dozens of occasions. It was a survivor.

And now it floated, carried along by a rapid stream of water, through a series of pipes running miles below the mountain's surface. The phone was in total darkness, but that didn't matter. It was busy, preoccupied with trying to send the last text message its owner had typed into it.

That had been *three* days ago—not six. Though it was still a long time. Long enough that things were starting to get dangerous.

The phone, unlike its owner, knew the exact time and date. But its time was running out. Its battery was getting pretty low. Three days of trying to send a text with no cellular service was enough to kill any battery, even the bigger, bulkier one built into the phone's impact-resistant case.

If the message had been cat videos, this whole thing would have been over two days ago.

But the phone was still active, still trying to transmit as it bumped along in the darkness under the mountain. It hadn't received any texts or calls or notifications in three days, and so its display hadn't come on, casting useless light into the darkness. It hadn't eaten up precious battery power displaying emojis or Facebook updates or dozens of calls from concerned colleagues or family members or the owner's boyfriend.

The battery was close to its end, though. The last remnants of energy were ebbing. It wouldn't be long now.

Suddenly, however, the phone was thrust out into daylight, and now it was bouncing along in a stream, with trees and sky and birds above. It ricocheted from a rock, spinning on the turbulent water's surface as it floated downstream. Its screen reflected the open sky above, dappled patterns of tree leaves and limbs reflecting from it, the soft shapes of clouds breaking up patches of blue.

If it had been alive, or aware, it might have welcomed the sunny day, instead of merely reflecting it back, passive on the outside.

But active on the inside.

Still no signal. Still trying to transmit. Still, the battery dwindled.

It was down to its last electrons, the last tiny bits of power ebbing away, when the signal came.

It wasn't much. Barely enough to generate a green bar—one of four. A half-bar. A quarter-bar, really. Not enough for a cat video. Barely enough for anything at all.

But enough for the text.

It finally went through. And just as it was finished, the battery gave up its life, taking the phone with it, just as the current was doing. The phone moved on, its work done. Maybe someday it would be reunited with its owner.

But it was doubtful.

Clara's last message now ricocheted from tower to tower, from tower to satellite, and from satellite to even more towers. No battery power needed, now. The signal had its own life, powered by the network of communication that blanketed the whole Earth.

And finally it landed, finding its mark, alerting the user with a chime or a chirp.

It was read—another user. Kyle. The boyfriend. The first contact in Clara's Favorites. A person she knew, trusted well enough, but might not have specifically chosen, had she not been in a hurry.

The message was interpreted. It was understood.

And then Kyle started to make frantic texts and calls of his own.

Mission accomplished, the phone bounced along with the current, until it was eventually wedged between two large stones.

It was, at least, very well protected by the phone case.

Dr. Dan Kotler—Archaeologist, occasional FBI Consultant, newly credentialed member of the Historic Crimes task force—was on a coffee break.

His third of the evening.

Though, he would admit, it wasn't much of a break if you took the work with you, which Kotler had all three times.

It wasn't that he was a workaholic. It was just that the current work was so *interesting*. Or perhaps *engrossing* was the better word. It seemed like most of the projects he'd become involved in over the past few years were of the sort to absorb every bit of his attention, to the point of obsession.

A hazard of the trade.

Over the past few years, as Kotler had started doing more and more consulting with the FBI, he'd more or less strayed from his work in academia. Which was too bad, because he frankly *loved* his work in academia. Or... well, he loved the work, if not academia itself. He and the established institutions were a bit at odds with each other these days. He was amicable, but the scientific community... not so much.

It might have something to do with the fact that Kotler was consistently getting involved in things that set current archaeological research on its ear.

In the past four years alone, Kotler had been instrumental in uncovering a Viking presence in Pueblo, Colorado; had found a potential site for the lost city of Atlantis; had been part of the exploration of a newly discovered Mayan city; and had helped to stop a criminal enterprise from using materials stolen from *Göbekli Tepe* to overthrow the world governments and shift the balance of power. He'd helped to stop bad guys from unleashing plagues, mind control devices, advanced stealth technology, and an army of cloned gods.

The usual.

It was at a point where even Kotler himself was having a hard time believing all the trouble one lone archaeologist could get involved in. If he'd had a whip and a fedora, there'd be movies made about him.

Instead, his trademarks tended to be a cup of hot coffee and an iPad stuffed with translations, photos, and 3D models.

The current research was an exploration of *Por-Bajin*, in the Tuva Republic.

Recent carbon dating had revealed that the enigmatic island structure was not an elaborate Uighur khan palace, as current theory proposed, but was instead a Manichaeist monastery, which had gone unused due to the khan being killed in an anti-Manichaeism uprising.

As you do.

The return of the region to the shamanistic tradition of Tengrism had spelled the end of the brief conversion to Manichaeism. And it had left behind a mystery that lingered since the site's discovery in the 19th century.

Until now.

A new approach to carbon dating the site had led

researchers to discover that it was built in 777, which was fascinating all on its own. The date put the structure's construction during the life and reign of Tengri Bögü Khan—the khan who had forced the region to switch from the traditional shamanistic Tengrism to Manichaeism. Which, inevitably, had led to the Khan being ousted and executed, as the region's faith was restored to "normal."

These details were intriguing and lent volumes of speculation and insight to potential solutions to the enigma of *Por-Bajin*.

But the reason the island fortress was currently occupying digital real estate on Kotler's iPad was because the link to Manichaeism indicated that the layout of the structure may have more meaning than anyone had first assumed. It may have been designed to convey a secret message—one that hinted at a long-lost trove of knowledge, treasure, and wonder.

Kotler simply loved troves of knowledge, treasure, and wonder.

He sipped coffee while seated at his usual table, in front of the window facing a busy Manhattan sidewalk. This was a cafe he frequented, just a few blocks from his high-rise apartment. The owners and wait staff knew him by name, and knew that he was prone to long hours spent pondering whatever was on his iPad. They kept his coffee cup full, bless them.

Kotler hadn't had the chance to spend much time here lately, thanks to his work with the FBI. There had been months of travel during the latest "case," and Kotler had found himself sleeping in uncomfortable, sometimes wretched conditions, occasionally dodging bullets or free-climbing his way out of death traps.

Again, the usual.

Kotler enjoyed the consulting work, however. Even the death traps. He spent a lot of time traveling, helping to keep nefarious people from doing despicable things, from using out-of-place history as a weapon or a tool for world domination or whatever dark purpose they had in mind. It was good and worthy work, worth the discomfort and the risks.

He enjoyed all of it all the more, though, because his girlfriend—Dr. Liz Ludlum—happened to be the current Director of Historic Crimes.

The two of them kept things strictly professional on the job, but just like the research he was studying now, Kotler tended to bring his work home with him. It was good to bring it home to someone who understood it and knew why he was doing it. Someone who understood that risk was part of the job, and that the job was worth doing, for the sake of making the world a safer place. Kotler couldn't be more appreciative of Liz's understanding.

She'd given him the cases, after all.

Well, him and his partner, Agent Roland Denzel—the FBI agent who had gotten Kotler into this line of work in the first place. And—though Denzel might be reluctant to admit it—Kotler's best friend in the world.

Their friendship wasn't lifelong. They'd only met a few years earlier. But they were bonded by battle, having faced life-threatening challenges together. They knew and trusted each other. And, Kotler believed, there were few who were more loyal, dedicated, and dependable than Agent Roland Denzel.

As if merely contemplating his name had conjured the man himself, Kotler blinked as he spotted Denzel passing by the coffee shop window. The agent stopped, checked his phone, and then entered the shop. He stood in the doorway, looking around until he spotted Kotler, then joined him at the little table.

"I figured I'd find you here, when you weren't at your place," Denzel said.

"Why here?" Kotler asked. "Why not the university? The museum?"

Denzel shrugged. "They don't like you there as much as people like you here. And Hemingway's was closed."

Hemingway's was Kotler's local pub of choice, and he had to admit that if the day had been just a little later, there was a good chance he'd be there. He had his own booth in that place as well. He tended to be a regular when he was in town.

Kotler smiled and laughed, shaking his head. "Something up?" He sipped from his coffee.

"You haven't answered your text messages or your phone calls."

Kotler nodded, placing the cup down next to his iPad. "Liz ordered me to turn it all off for a couple of days." He grinned, leaning back slightly. "I'm not allowed to play with you right now."

Liz Ludlum—*Dr.* Liz Ludlum—the Director of Historic Crimes, had been pretty busy lately. While still managing to keep the entire operation running, she was working long hours to get the new task force organized and populated with agents from the entire alphabet of US government law enforcement. She also spent most of her days courting experts from nearly every field.

Historic Crimes was a new division of law enforcement itself—an inter-agency partnership run by a joint civilian and government oversight committee. Which, of course, meant it was a beast to organize and run.

The agency's motto was *Ad serve historia, praesidio homnibus.*

To serve history, and protect humanity.

No small endeavor.

Denzel had been asked to be her second-in-command for the task force. So far, he'd dragged his feet on accepting, though it seemed a natural fit. Kotler wasn't sure why his friend was reluctant, and he respected him too much to ask. Denzel was a private person, and until he was ready to share, he wouldn't. No sense poking around until he was ready.

"She's the one who had me find you," Denzel replied. "Something's come up. An agent's gone missing. One of the civilian agents."

Kotler considered this. "Missing persons? Not typically my thing."

"It's kind of an all-hands thing," Denzel shrugged. "But you've been requested. There was a text message, and it contains something that made Ludlum think it might be best to bring you in."

"Text message?" Kotler asked.

Denzel took out his phone and showed a screenshot to Kotler. "This was sent to the agent's boyfriend."

KYLE, *I need help! Still in Los Lunas. Found the Pit. Decalogue translations plus quantum encrypt totally worked. There's a man with a face tattoo chasing me. He's blocking every way out. No signal, so I'm hoping you get this. SEND HELP!*

KOTLER LOOKED up from the message, surprised.

"You recognize it?" Denzel asked. "The deca-what'sit?"

"The *Decalogue* stone in Los Lunas?" Kotler replied. He shook his head. "It's sometimes called the *Mystery* stone. It's... well, to be frank, it's considered by most academics and researchers to be a fraud, perpetrated by Frank Hibbins back in the 30s."

Denzel nodded. "And what do you think?"

Kotler considered this, shaking his head. "I've never been

sure. Hibbins had a... well, let's say a bad history. He'd been caught faking data to support his theories. Hibbins and others claimed the writing on the Decalogue stone was Paleo-Hebrew, or maybe Cypriotic Greek. Both languages that should have no place in New Mexico at that time, or any other, really. I've seen photos of the stone. The characters could be Phoenician, but again... not something you'd expect to find in New Mexico in the 30s." He shook his head again. "I've never looked that closely at it. Never seen it in person."

Denzel nodded. "Well, you're going to have your chance. Ludlum wants us both on a plane to New Mexico this afternoon."

Kotler huffed, blowing a breath out through pursed lips. "I'll swing by my place and get my gear. Anyone going with us on this one?"

Denzel scowled and shook his head again. "Yeah," he said. "This time we're bringing someone along."

Agent Eric Symon was seated in Director Ludlum's office, looking past her empty desk at the Manhattan skyline. To his left was Agent Julia Mayher.

The two of them had been partners in the FBI for some time now, brought together on the hunt for Alex Kayne—the brilliant creator of an advanced AI that someone in the government wanted badly enough to put nearly every government law enforcement agency on the case.

Kayne was one of the most wanted fugitives Symon had ever hunted.

She was also innocent.

That was what Symon believed, at any rate, after pursuing her for months. He knew her pretty well, by this point. She'd managed to slip through his fingers on more than one occasion.

Beyond that, however, he knew that at any time she could disappear off of the face of the planet, wipe any and all records of her existence clean, and be nothing but a memory in a heartbeat—and yet, she stuck around, risking her freedom and her life to help bring justice to the disenfranchised.

Symon would pursue her, and he would arrest her. He'd do his job, no question. But he couldn't help believing that she was innocent. It was an instinct. Something about her case didn't click for him—his sense of fugitives was honed by hundreds of man-hours on hundreds of man-hunts. And there was something about Kayne's case that didn't fit.

He suspected she was being framed.

And he couldn't help but also suspect that Alex Kayne might be the biggest reason—maybe even the sole reason—that he and Agent Mayher had been offered a slot in Historic Crimes.

It was no secret that Kayne was the fugitive everyone wanted. Kayne... and QuIEK—the Quantum Integrated Encryption Key. Pronounced "quake" to those in the know, which wasn't many.

Dangerous and powerful, QuIEK was on every government's Christmas wish list. Everyone wanted it. Which meant that everyone wanted Kayne.

Symon was one of the few people to ever get close enough to Kayne to actually lay hands on her. Of course, she'd escaped—immediately, and in a way that was kind of embarrassing for Symon and his team.

She'd made her escape, and was in the wind, but still stuck around to help a young amputee recover her prototype prosthetic arm. She'd nearly been caught a dozen times, because of that choice, but had stuck around anyway, eventually setting things right.

It was the kind of thing Alex Kayne just *did*. Again and

again. Putting herself and her freedom at risk for strangers who had suffered injustice. It made it tough to think of her as being the traitor and murderer she was claimed to be.

That first encounter with her had told Symon a lot. It had also established a relationship between the two of them that he was sure his superiors would not appreciate.

She'd been in contact with him ever since they'd met.

Nothing untoward. Nothing physical, or even romantic. He couldn't even say they were friends, per se. But she contacted him frequently, shared data with him, sent him leads, sometimes even wrapped bad guys up in a nice, neat package for him to arrest.

It was a weird sort of relationship. But it had its perks.

Kayne *could* be the reason that Symon and Mayher were invited to play in the new sandbox that Historic Crimes had opened up. In fact, it seemed probable. But Symon had his own reasons for joining the team. Reasons he hadn't yet revealed to anyone, even his partner.

He glanced at Mayher, who was fidgeting with her suit jacket.

"Relax," he smiled. "You'll love Director Ludlum."

"I've met her," Mayher said sourly, then shook her head. "*Virtually.*"

"She's a lot more three-dimensional in person," Symon said.

Mayher looked as if she were about to respond when Director Ludlum herself entered the room, smiled as a greeting, and settled into her seat behind the big desk.

Ludlum always seemed to Symon to be too young for her role. A brilliant, young black woman in her mid-thirties, Ludlum had risen quickly through the ranks of first the NYPD and then the FBI, becoming head of Forensics for each, respectively. She'd worked with the FBI as part of it's budding new program—Historic Crimes—an offshoot of their White Collar division, with a charter to take on cases involving "out-of-place history" that might threaten the US or even the world.

The task force had quite a track record. And so did Ludlum. She'd been directly responsible for dozens of saves, keeping the world from being thrown into plagues or war or worse.

When the former Historic Crimes Director was murdered, Ludlum was elevated to take her place. And it seemed she'd been the best choice for the role. She'd already moved metaphorical mountains to get the new and improved Historic Crimes running like a finely tuned machine.

Symon had done his due diligence and research into Ludlum. She might seem young, but she'd proven herself to be more than up to the task of leading this fledgling law enforcement agency and task force. She was new, still learning, but she was also as tough and fierce as she was smart. She could handle herself, and she could handle the task force.

Symon was a fan.

"Thank you for meeting with me," Ludlum smiled, taking her seat at the desk. She leaned forward on her elbows. "I know you had to fly in from Chicago."

Symon shook his head. "It's not a problem. We'd run into a dead end there, anyway. The case wrapped up, and Kayne moved on."

Ludlum nodded. "Alex Kayne. She's pretty good at giving everyone the slip."

"The best I've ever seen," Symon replied.

"You sound like you admire her?" Ludlum smiled.

Symon's eyes widened slightly. "No, I... I mean, I don't *underestimate* her."

He glanced quickly at Mayher, who had pursed her lips and was shaking her head slightly.

Ludlum turned to Mayher next. "And Agent Mayher, it's good to finally meet in person."

"Thank you Director, I feel the same way."

Ludlum rolled her eyes. "Please call me Liz. No one does anymore, and I'm starting to miss it."

Mayher again glanced at Symon and back to Ludlum. "I... don't think that would be appropriate, ma'am."

Ludlum laughed. "No, I guess not. How about just when we're behind closed doors?" She watched the both of them and smiled as she continued. "Well, we might as well get down to business. Agent Symon, I have something I'd like you to get to Alex Kayne."

Symon nodded. He suspected he might end up being the go-between for Historic Crimes and Kayne. It wasn't the role he'd signed up for, and he genuinely hoped it wouldn't be the only thing he was here to do. But he also knew that Ludlum and her superiors saw Kayne as an asset, to the point of granting her status as a Confidential Informant.

Kayne was still a fugitive. If Symon or any other agent could swing it, she'd be arrested and put in a very deep hole until she surrendered QuIEK to the government. But having her as a CI meant that they could legitimately interact with her without fear of professional or legal repercussions. It was the closest to granting her a pardon as they were going to get, without her turning over QuIEK.

It would have to do.

"I'll do what I can. I don't exactly have her on speed dial."

Ludlum nodded. "I understand. I want you to pass along an email I'm forwarding to you. It contains everything we know about a civilian agent, Dr. Clara Rivers. She went missing a few days ago, and the only lead we have is a pretty cryptic text message she sent to her boyfriend." Ludlum turned to her computer and tapped a few keys, then nodded to the two agents.

Symon took out his phone and checked email, as did Mayher. He read the message, then looked up at Ludlum.

"You can see why I thought of Kayne," she said.

"*Quantum encrypt?*" Symon asked. "As in quantum *encryption?*"

"That's a principal part of Kayne's AI, isn't it?" Ludlum asked. "The Q-u-I in QuIEK?"

"It is," Symon nodded. "Though it's not entirely uncommon. It's something a lot of researchers are working with. An entire field of research, really."

"A field that Alex Kayne has already mastered," Ludlum replied. "And a good enough excuse to get her involved." She said this last with a glint in her eye.

"You... are you just trying to find an excuse to engage her?" Symon asked.

Ludlum shook her head. "Not entirely. I really did think of her first, when this came up. But we haven't worked with you *or* her yet. All of this," she motioned to the offices around her, the brand new Historic Crimes HQ, in the Danielle Brown Memorial Building. "It's *all* new. And right now, I'm not sure how everyone is going to work together. So I need cases. Test cases. And, since Clara Rivers is one of our own agents, this seems like a good enough reason to pull in all the troops. Everyone who isn't already assigned to a case is being put on this one. Top priority."

Symon again looked quickly to Mayher, then back to Ludlum. "Everyone," he said flatly.

Ludlum studied him for a moment. "I know you have some... history... with Agent Denzel, and with Dr. Kotler."

"I'm sorry," Symon said. "I know you and Dr. Kotler have a relationship."

She nodded. "It can get a little complicated. But the thing is, Dan is the best there is at what he does. There's a component of this case that involves his specialty. He seems to work best when he has Agent Denzel there to keep him on track. So... they're involved. I gave them the case this morning, before you arrived. Denzel is running it. And I want you and Agent Mayher to meet with them to New Mexico."

Symon blew out a breath. "Yes ma'am," he said.

Ludlum shuddered. "I kind of hate being called *ma'am*, too."

"I think protocol is to call you 'sir,' if that helps," Mayher replied, smiling.

Ludlum made a gagging noise, shaking her head. "*Ma'am* it is, then. Or Director. But in here, doors closed... it's *Liz*."

She squinted at Mayher, who laughed lightly, nodding. "Liz it is, then."

Ludlum smiled and stood, and Symon and Mayher joined her. "I've had flights arranged, and there's a car waiting for you. You'll meet Agent Denzel and Dr. Kotler in New Mexico. Between now and then, Agent Symon... if you can get some details to Alex Kayne, I think it could help. I'd like to make her a part of this, somehow."

"Does she get a pass?" Symon asked. "If she comes in on this, do we arrest her?"

"That's the job," Ludlum said, but there was something in her expression.

She believes me, Symon realized. *She believes me when I say that Kayne is innocent.*

Which, ultimately, was Symon's biggest reason for taking the job with Historic Crimes in the first place.

If he had any shot at helping to clear Kayne's name, it was going to be here, with this new agency. Kayne was still a fugitive, still radioactive as long as she was on the run with QuIEK under her control. But here, as part of Historic Crimes, Symon thought he could get the breathing room and resources he needed to clear her. To make things right for *her* for once.

He felt like it was the best shot Kayne had, and he was the only one who could do it.

If he didn't have to arrest her first.

CHAPTER TWO

Alex Kayne was siting in a bistro in Los Lunas, New Mexico, watching as a young couple toyed with playing chess at one of the rounder cafe tables. Neither of them seemed to really understand the rules of the game, but they were moving pieces and smiling and laughing. Alex found it kind of nice. Good moments were her secret passion—she took them wherever and whenever she could find them.

There was music playing overhead, and the crowd, though light, was chatting and creating a nice ambience. Alex had a cup of coffee and a chicken salad sandwich in front of her, set askew from the laptop that was tapped into every security camera, mobile phone, smart tablet, and traffic cam within ten blocks of the place.

She was watching more than an amateur chess match.

QuIEK—pronounced "quake," because Alex was clever and liked acronyms—was the reason Alex was hiding out, paranoid and on the run, rather than enjoying a view of the San Francisco Bay from her high-rise apartment. Or maybe playing faux chess with a partner of her own.

The Quantum Integrated Encryption Key was an AI of her own design, built to secure data at a level that no one on Earth could ever crack. Except it was also capable of *bypassing* any digital security system on the planet with astounding ease—which made it of keen interest to governments worldwide. Including the US government, which currently had Alex Kayne at the top of every most-wanted list imaginable, framed for treason and murder.

She was innocent. But try telling that to the US alphabet agencies.

Innocent or not, on the lam or not, Alex had never been able to stomach injustice—for herself, or for anyone else. Which was why she now traveled the country, using QuIEK to help bring justice for the disenfranchised and the forgotten. She spent her days—her whole *life*, really—peering into the cold case files of the FBI and other agencies, finding people who needed someone, *anyone*, who was willing and able to help them.

She did help. And she did bring justice to those who needed it most. But it meant that she could never put down roots, never call any place home for more than a quick layover. And never without putting herself in danger of being caught at any minute.

Sitting in this little bistro in New Mexico was a direct result of Alex's drive to help people who needed her most. Though this time, it was less about helping the disenfranchised and more about doing Agent Eric Symon a favor.

She kind of owed him one. Maybe a dozen.

When Symon had reached out to her through their usual back channels, he'd given her the full run-down of what was happening in Los Lunas. A civilian agent of the Historic Crimes task force was missing, under some pretty weird circumstances, and the phrase "quantum encrypt" had rung bells all over the place. Bells that reminded everyone of Alex Kayne and QuIEK.

So, here she was, risking being caught and arrested once again, trying to piece out what the mysterious text message from Dr. Clara Rivers meant.

So far, it made no real sense.

KYLE, I need help! Still in Los Lunas. Found the Pit. Decalogue translations plus quantum encrypt totally worked. There's a man with a face tattoo chasing me. He's blocking every way out. No signal so I'm hoping you get this. SEND HELP!

ALL OF THIS was out of context, and even the boyfriend—Kyle—wasn't entirely sure what all of it meant. He knew that Clara had gone to Los Lunas, knew that she was hunting for something there, and he was able to tell them that Clara had sent him emails and text messages since she'd left. He shared all of this with Historic Crimes.

Clara had recently started looking into translations of the Decalogue stone, Kyle revealed, but he wasn't sure why. Something about a conversation she'd had with a local.

He also wasn't sure what she meant by "quantum encrypt." He knew she "worked in computers," and the phrase "quantum" was one he thought was familiar. Beyond that, however, Kyle showed a remarkably shallow insight into his girlfriend or her work.

So, there were a few answers, but a whole lot of questions.

The majority of information Alex had to work from was confined in the text itself. She'd just have to piece her way through it, a phrase a time, like brute-force hacking from the old days.

She'd never actually been a hacker, but QuIEK gave everyone the impression that she was. In reality, she'd just made some fairly brilliant intuitive leaps while creating her encryption software. Leaps that she hadn't documented, which turned out to be a good thing. She was the sole living person who understood how QuIEK functioned. So as long as she could stay out of the hands of law enforcement, the world was a safer, more secure place.

It meant living a pretty lonely life. But given the alternative —a world where one government had unlimited power over all others—it was worth the sacrifice.

She had to believe that. She it to herself as often as she could stand it.

She shook her head. Time to focus. One phrase at a time.

Los Lunas was easy enough. The town was small, only about 15,000 people. As small towns went it was... well... one of them. No one was going to mistake the place as a major metropolitan area anytime soon, but there were nice spots— little niches like this bistro, where she could hide out in plain sight. There were some hotels and few Airbnbs available. Not exactly five-star accommodations, but far from being hovels in the dirt.

So far, though, there wasn't much to the town itself that might explain why Dr. Rivers had disappeared.

Thanks to some Googling and sniffing around in the Historic Crimes database, *Decalogue translations* now made more sense. According to Historic Crimes' resident super-archaeologist, Dr. Dan Kotler, it was a stone with ancient writing on it, "possibly Phoenician or Cypriot Greek." Though Dr. Kotler seemed to think it had a better chance of being Paleo-Hebrew.

Alex had Googled all of *that*, too, discovering that "Cypriot Greek" was a dialect of modern Greek, from Cyprus, and was likely the result of Cyprus being cut off from the rest of the Greek world from the 7th to 10th century. Basically, it was a variant of what would become modern Greek, complete with its own vocabulary, syntax, etc.

It was *all* Greek to Alex, either way. She couldn't parse anything useful from the overview of the Decalogue stone. Maybe with time she'd start to see connections, but for now, she was willing to leave that particular mystery to Dr. Kotler.

The thing that had her intrigued and paying close attention to the text message, though, was the phrase "quantum encrypt."

Alex, like Director Ludlum and everyone else, assumed this was shorthand for "quantum encryption." And this had Alex running translations and algorithms on the Decalogue text in QuIEK, to see what might pop up.

So far, it was a big, fat nothing. But she let the program run. Maybe it would turn something up, eventually.

This part of Alex's work could be done from literally anywhere on Earth, which would have negated the risk of being out in public in a small town where she knew for a fact there was a bunch of FBI and other US law enforcement folks turning over stones and peering into every crevice.

The risk of being here was high to the point of being nuts.

But Alex's work also tended to include a bit of hands-on, with her doing everything from breaking and entering to masquerading as someone else, so she could pick up crucial information that might not be available in a digital database. Paper and word of mouth were QuIEK's kryptonite. So it was sometimes up to Alex to sniff out non-digital details.

She could never be entirely sure when those hands-on skills would be needed, or when she'd need to dig through someone's garbage or pilfer through their file cabinets. So, here she was, risking everything, just in case. It was what she did for her clients. Even clients she hadn't actually met.

Although for once, her "client" was Agent Eric Symon.

He was the best there was at hunting fugitives. He'd tracked down some of the most elusive escape artists in recent history. And he'd almost gotten his hands on Alex Kayne as well. She'd just been more paranoid and prepared than he'd bargained for, at the time.

Being on the run is a lonely business, however. Alex had very few actual relationships these days. And so, like a lot of fugitives before her, she'd formed a bond with her pursuer.

Nothing too fancy, and certainly not romantic—just some text messages and the occasional nudge-nudge-wink-wink when it came to handing over criminals that Alex had helped to take down. For the most part, Alex would do all the heavy lifting of finding dirt on someone who was a real piece of pond scum, and then hand them over to Symon and the FBI, wrapped up neat and tidy with a bow on top.

She was good with Symon getting credit for her work. She knew Symon believed that she was innocent of the charges against her. She knew as well that Symon was actively looking for ways to clear her name. But she didn't let any of this stuff fool her.

Symon would arrest her, first chance he got. He wouldn't hold back. One slip, and she'd be in the hole.

That said, he was putting a lot on the line as well, just working with her, even if it was remotely. She *was* a fugitive, after all. Innocent or not, he was occasionally aiding and abetting.

So, in the rare event that he reached out asking for her help with one of his cases, she was fine with helping him. To a point. Actually, this was the first time he'd ever done so—how could she refuse?

Alex looked away from the chess match and scanned through lines of translation and on screen messages from

QuIEK. The translations went fine—QuIEK had tapped into thousands of linguistic databases at universities and museums all over the world, and had compiled what would probably turn out to be the most thorough and accurate translation of the Decalogue on the planet. That was cool.

It just wasn't *useful*.

There was something missing. This couldn't be purely about translation—others had done that work before her, and they were at least experts on the archaeology of the whole thing. Using quantum encryption to do her own translation was really sort of overkill, to a nearly infinite degree.

But there was more here than this surface stuff. There had to be. And for nails like this, QuIEK was Alex's hammer.

Alex ran through the text message again, noting each little piece and part, trying to make it work in some kind of context— of course, context was the one thing she was missing. But maybe there was something in this that would click. Some random connection she'd make, just by softening her focus and letting things shift around and gel in her conciseness.

There were just so many unanswered questions.

What did Clara mean by "a man with a face tattoo?" What about "the pit?" What was it, and why was she searching for it? How had the Decalogue Stone become mixed up in all of this?

Kyle hadn't known the answers to any of these questions. No clue. He'd heard Clara mention "the pit," but it was in passing, sort of a quick blur of enthusiasm she'd blurted out at dinner one evening.

When they found her, Alex was thinking she should recommend that Clara find a new boyfriend. Kyle didn't seem to be the attentive type.

Actually, as Alex thought about it, the word "pit" had been capitalized, like a proper noun.

Not a *pit*... the *Pit*.

Was that a clue?

Alex opened a new window and started running a scan, using QuIEK to conduct a context trace between a variety of databases, public and otherwise. Being able to phase through even the most secure government databases like they were search results on Google had its advantages.

She was looking for anything in those databases that was called "the Pit," with a connection to New Mexico, and Los Lunas in particular.

It took only seconds, and QuIEK returned results from an archival database on the US Army's servers—highly classified stuff.

The records went back to the forties, but had been updated as recently as the late 90s, with notes and scientific documentation.

That got Alex's interest.

The "Pit" had started as an off-books project in the 1940s that paralleled development of the Manhattan Project, which was being run just two hours away from Los Lunas, in Los Alamos. Unlike its more famous sibling, the Pit continued as an ongoing research project well after the end of the World War II, as a means of developing new technology spun from the findings and research of Robert Oppenheimer and his team, as well as from captured Nazi tech. The really weird, almost unbelievable Nazi tech that Alex had only heard of from shows like *Ancient Aliens*.

Some research was absurd—far-fetched ideas like interdimensional travel along "threads" woven throughout reality, or superhuman capabilities such as the transference of memories by touch. Other avenues were more practical, from a scientific standpoint, like faster-than-light travel facilitated by coherent beams of energy, or cryogenic stasis. This sort of tech was actually in development *now*.

Science fiction wasn't as sci-fi as it used to be.

From the documents she was recovering, many of which were labeled "Classified," it looked like the Pit had been active as a black operation for fifty years before it suddenly went dark in the 1990s. Over that time, tech recovered from Nazis subtly shifted to tech recovered from the Soviets, from China, from fringe science groups, and a few sources labeled simply "Classified Source." Nothing alarming there.

Adding to the weirdness of interdimensional travel and trans-osmosis, the files started detailing such terrifying alt-science gems as human cloning, designer gene therapy, and super viruses. The term "technology" expanded to included not only circuits and wires but pixels and bits, and finally bio-enhancement and genetics. And out of the research and experiments conducted in the facility came references to some pretty chilling use-cases and applications for what they were finding.

It was like reading a wish list from Satan.

There was no indication as to why the Pit stopped operating in the 90s. Records just *stopped*. No follow-up, beyond a few inquiries from top brass in the military. And most of those seemed to be carefully worded versions of "is this thing dead yet?"

Essentially, from around 1996, it was radio silence. Nothing useful, no files to find. Nothing to see here.

Still, this seemed like a significant enough lead to Alex.

She dutifully sent everything she had to Agent Symon, then packed up her laptop and left the bistro behind. Most of what she'd just shared was classified information, but she'd taken precautions, using QuIEK to grant access to these files. Anyone who bothered to check would see that Historic Crimes suddenly had some pretty significant clearance.

Call it my gift to Erics' new bosses, Alex thought.

So they should be covered. And for now, it was time to put some distance between her and this spot.

She'd been here too long as it was.

Being out in public like this wasn't really necessary—she could do what she did from any place that had internet access. It was just that being a fugitive was a pretty rough and lonely life. Being able to sit in a cafe or bookshop, like a normal person, sipping coffee and eating a sandwich, just *being there* for an hour or two here and there... it was...

Necessary.

And dangerous, for sure. She'd been spotted and nearly captured before, thanks to someone randomly recognizing her in public. But for her own sake, for her mental health, spending some time with the three-dimensional people—even if it was at arm's length—it was a need and a must. It kept her grounded. Kept her sane. It was worth the risk.

Still, she did have escape routes mapped out in all directions, and backup plans for her backup plans. It was her way.

Paranoia—never leave home without it.

She was using one of those pre-planned escape routes now, catching a string of Ubers to help her bounce across the city in hops. This sort of circuitous route was time consuming, but essential. When she finally landed in the Airbnb across town— really only five blocks from where she'd been sitting, but more than an hour's drive by her route—she'd accumulated about sixty miles of travel and swapped rides dozens of times. QuIEK kept all of this moving, kept traffic lights tuned for her passing, kept security and ATM cameras fritzed out as she passed. There would be no record of her. She was a ghost here.

It was paranoia evolved to an art form, for sure. But it was necessary. It kept her out of some deep, dark pit somewhere— maybe a place like *the* Pit—imprisoned until she agreed to hand over QuIEK. Maybe even beyond that.

She was a catch, after all. Brains, beauty, a penchant for thinking twenty steps ahead—the whole package.

By the time she reached "home," however, she'd gotten a response from Agent Symon.

Someone wants to chat with you, if you're up for it, the text message read.

You know how much I love meeting strangers, Alex replied.

The three little dots appeared.

Eric had been watching and waiting for her.

It made her smile, amused. Maybe even a little touched, though she knew it was more likely that Symon saw this as important for the case, rather than eagerly awaiting her response.

He's practically family, now that you're doing some work for Historic Crimes. It's Dr. Dan Kotler. He's with me here at the hotel. He read the stuff you sent over, and he thinks you're on to something. He wants to discuss some ideas with you. Up to chat with him?

Alex blinked at her phone, dropping it to her side for a moment as she stepped out onto the patio of the rental house. Her view was a range of mountains in the distance, a blue sky that was crystalline in its clarity. The air was crips and cool, thanks to Fall descending on the region. Maybe even a little too chilly. She hugged her arms to her chest.

There was no reason to chat with Dr. Kotler.

Except...

She knew that Dr. Kotler and Agent Denzel were the ones who had brought down FBI Director Crispen, half a decade earlier. That had nothing to do with Alex, and was no skin off her nose. Except for the fact that it was that series of events which had put Agent Eric Symon's career in a tailspin. He was only just recovering from all of it, getting his reputation back slowly. There was still some distrust of him at the FBI, despite being cleared of all wrongdoing.

Kotler and Denzel had basically put Symon in a dark place for a long time. It was a little too relatable, even if mostly from a metaphorical sense.

Alex knew that Kotler and Denzel hadn't done anything intentional or malicious. And hell, Agent Symon seemed to be working past his own hangups about the two, at least enough to work with them.

Such a professional, Alex thought. *He'd never let a grudge keep him from doing his job. Never do anything that personal.*

She paused. *I would, though. I guess I'm kind of holding a grudge on his behalf.*

She smiled, then laughed, then shook her head.

All of this might be reason enough to talk to Dr. Kotler, to size him up and see what he was all about.

She looked at her phone again and typed her reply.

I'll talk to him. Give him this URL.

She typed in a string of numbers and characters that would lead Dr. Kotler to a video chat room. It was completely secure, encrypted with the most advanced AI software on the planet. When their talk was done, it would cease to exist.

She followed that text with a specific time for the chat, and when she was done, she started dressing the room. She hung blankets to form a sound barrier all around her laptop, as well as to hide the art and decor of the room.

It was possible, she knew, to identify rooms like this one from online listings. Room decor could act like a fingerprint, allowing the FBI to run an image recognition search from a video still, comparing it to online listings until it started producing matches. It would be time consuming, without the aid of QuIEK, but it could be done. And any lead might be enough to put them closer to her than she preferred.

She wouldn't take any chances.

She also turned on a recording of cityscape sounds from Los Angeles. More camouflage, in case someone tried audio forensics, matching her soundscape to a database of audio files recorded in various locations. Another long, tedious route to tracking a fugitive that she could do in seconds. But someone could get lucky, especially if they assumed she was in Los Lunas.

With the fake audio track running, though, anyone monitoring and analyzing the audio would be thrown off of her trail. Which was just how she liked it.

After more preparation, and way more paranoia, she was finally ready for her chat with Dr. Kotler.

She sat facing her laptop, which was connected to a hotspot that was then routed through a virtual network of her own design, a system she referred to as "Smokescreen," with modules and relays stashed in spots all over the country. If it were possible for anyone to trace the video chat from the URL she'd provided—*which it was not*—they'd have a hard time pinning down even a region of the country, much less her exact location. She could be in Poughkeepsie or on the moon, for all anyone knew.

Feeling secure, she waited. She was curious what the archaeologist had to say. Sitting there, waiting, the whole thing felt very momentous—as if two protagonists were about to meet in a first-ever crossover.

Soon enough the wait was over, there was a chime from the site, and Alex Kayne clicked the button to start the call.

Dr. Dan Kotler appeared on screen.

KOTLER HAD CLOSED himself off in his hotel room, pulling the curtains and even playing some music for white noise.

From what he'd learned about Alex Kayne, she was incredibly intelligent, unendingly resourceful, and paranoid to a level that would make conspiracy theorists look like Instagram celebrities. He wanted her to feel comfortable talking to him, but he knew it would take time. Chatting with her in private was his first, best guess at where to start.

Of course, it would help if Agent Symon were a little more forthcoming with details—and a little less passive-aggressive.

Liz had warned Kotler that the Agent might not be...

How did she put it?

"As warmly receptive to you as everyone else is."

Kotler had laughed. "Right. Everyone I meet considers me their bestie. Academia practically has me blacklisted, and half the archaeology community wants to strangle me."

"No more than Director Crispen might want to. I'm sorry... *former* Director Crispen."

Kotler blinked.

Matthew Crispen had been the Director of the Manhattan branch of the FBI when Kotler had first started working with the agency. Though "working with the agency" might be something of a stretch. Kotler had more or less been extorted into helping the FBI track down a terrorist cell that had stolen an ancient medallion. Crispen had been tied to aiding the organization, and to playing a role in the kidnapping of Kotler's former girlfriend—Dr. Evelyn Horelica.

The kidnapping, Kotler's recruitment, his entire role in the investigation had all been part of the ruse meant to frame him for Crispen's own crimes.

In the end, Kotler had met and teamed up with Agent Roland Denzel, and the two of them had managed to stop a terrorist attack that would have killed millions. They recovered both Kotler's ex and the stolen Coelho Medallion, and a partnership was born.

Things had come together remarkably well for Kotler. The entire affair had led to him becoming a full-time consultant for the FBI, and a founding member of Historic Crimes.

But it had also put Director Matthew Crispen in prison.

"What does Crispen have to do with Agent Symon?" Kotler had asked.

Liz sighed. "Symon was Crispen's golden boy. He recruited Agent Symon into the FBI and was grooming him for big things. Symon was... *is*... the best fugitive hunter in the Bureau, but his career got derailed after Crispen was arrested. He was accused of collaborating with Crispen, and it took years to clear his name. He's only just recovering."

Kotler considered this. It was sobering, to learn that Agent Symon had borne the fallout of Crispen's arrest. Kotler had never even considered that someone else in the Bureau might have been negatively impacted by Crispen's crimes.

He felt terrible for what the agent had gone through.

But he couldn't be blamed for it. That was just absurd.

Except...

Kotler sighed. He knew as well as anyone that logic and reason had little to do with grudges like these. It might be irrational, but blaming Kotler for his miseries was a pretty natural outcome for Agent Symon. It might not be fair, but Kotler figured it was at least understandable.

It did explain why Symon seemed so cold toward him and Agent Denzel.

Kotler had made a note to circle up with Roland later, and maybe the two of them could take Symon out for a drink. Coffee. Or something stronger. Maybe find a way to set the record straight at least, clear the air if not make things right.

For now, however, Kotler had a video chat ahead of him, with perhaps one of the most intriguing women he'd heard of in a long time. He had no idea what to expect—the briefing he'd gotten on Alex Kayne had definitely piqued his interest, though. From everything he'd learned, she was brilliant and clever. She had, after all, managed to elude the FBI's best fugitive hunter, not to mention every law enforcement agency in the world, and stay out of a cell for more than two years running.

Impressive work. Definitely someone Kotler had to meet.

Agent Symon had sent Kotler the URL in a text message, and Kotler opened it now from the Messages app on his iPad. The screen was black for a moment, and then the face of an attractive woman appeared. She was sitting in...

Kotler blinked.

"Are... are you in a blanket fort?" he asked.

The woman on screen also blinked, then laughed. She cleared her throat and shook her head. "No. But points for thinking out of the box, Dr. Kotler. Of course, going by your FBI profile, thinking out of the box is kind of your thing, isn't it?"

Kotler smiled. "No more than you, I hear. I've read your file, too. Impressive. Your use of quantum states for hyperparallel processing is pretty inspired."

Kayne looked impressed. "You say that like you understand what it means."

Kotler grinned. "I have a second PhD, in Quantum Mechanics."

Kayne smiled. "I know. Polymath. Pretty cool. You're also a savant with reading body language, I hear."

Kotler blinked. "That made it into the file? I thought most people thought it was a myth."

"It made it into emails," she replied. "And text messages. And a few personal journal entries."

Kotler's eyebrows went up, and he felt a strange chill in his guts. He dismissed it. From what he'd learned, Kayne certainly had the ability to snoop into personal files and private communications. And, apparently, her morals were flexible enough to allow it.

How could he blame her? This was a woman whose existence depended on knowing more than everyone else, at all times. Kotler tried to imagine what he would do, if he were in her position. He couldn't say that he'd stick around helping people, out of the kindness of his heart. He loved people—loved humanity—but mostly as a subject.

He was pretty sure he'd be firmly ensconced some place off the map and off the grid, with no extradition treaty.

Kotler nodded at the screen, still studying her face. He could see that she was trying to remain controlled, keeping her features neutral. "Face lying," he called it. But that was fine. Ironic, but fine.

After all, she could use her super power to know intimate things about *him*. He could hardly be blamed for gleaning as much as he could from her facial twitches, the hold of her shoulders, the rigidity of how she was sitting.

She was keeping herself in check, but still screaming a lot about herself, without even realizing.

Kotler smiled. This seemed to be going well, though Kayne was being a little stand-offish. He thought he knew why. Aside from being a fugitive, she also had very limited contact. And one of those she related to the most was Agent Eric Symon.

She would know that Kotler played a role in the events that had put Symon's career off track.

"I've seen other work in quantum encryption," Kotler said, "but nothing like what you've done with Quick."

"*Quake*," she corrected, then paused. "Although now that you say it, maybe I *should* have gone with *quick*. It probably would make more sense, considering. I tend to have to make a fast exit."

Kotler chuckled. "Oh, I don't know. Given how you've shaken things up, *quake* works just as well."

She returned a light laugh, then seemed to hesitate, inhaling and sighing. "Ok, so we've had a nice little introduction here. I know Eric has shown you the work I did, deciphering the content of that text. What do you need me to do for you?"

Kotler shook his head, smiling. "It's not like that. I didn't want to talk about what you can do for *me*. I wanted to ask what I could do for *you*."

She blinked. "What... do you mean?"

"You tracked down the site in Los Lunas. The Pit. Roland—Agent Denzel—is putting together an expedition to that facility. Agent Symon and Agent Mayher are tagging along. But from what I've learned about you, I'd think you would want to be there as well."

She laughed again. "Yeah, pretty impossible. I don't have any issues with sneaking into a top secret military base, defunct or otherwise. But unfortunately I'm not in a position to do it with a bunch of FBI agents surrounding me. I'd mostly end up being a permanent resident at some *other* top secret government facility."

"Not just FBI," Kotler said.

"Excuse me?" Kayne replied.

"It's not just FBI. Historic Crimes is a multi-agency task force. There are a couple of CIA agents, one NSA agent, and some people who work for agencies I haven't even heard of. Plus the civilian operatives, like me and Dr. Rivers."

"All the more reason to avoid the place, then," Kayne replied, her expression strange.

Kotler nodded. "I agree. Still, I've seen your file. You might be a bigger asset than any of them. We have no idea what's in that place—as you pointed out, the records go cold in the 90s.

The only hint was the phrase 'quantum encrypt,' which is your bailiwick. That's a lot of unknowns, and I'm not big on going into situations with so little foreknowledge. Personally, I'd like to have you there."

"Again," Kayne replied, spreading her hands and leaning back, "not really possible. Not with so many people ready to arrest me on the spot."

"Ready to arrest Alex Kayne," Kotler said.

"Right," Kayne replied.

"But not Dr. Alicia Carter."

Kayne shook her head. "Who's that?"

Kotler laughed. "Well, *you*, if you do the work to set up her identity."

Kayne stared at him. "You want me to come on this little mission in disguise? With an assumed identity?"

"Isn't it something you've done before?" Kotler asked.

"Sure," Kayne replied. "Something I do almost daily. Just... not under these circumstances."

Kotler nodded, hesitated, then said, "I looked over the files you found, about the Pit. The project was abandoned in the 90s, but even for that decade, things were pretty advanced. Half of what you sent us is actually classified information. I don't think the agents have realized it yet."

"I wouldn't tell them," Kayne warned.

Kotler chuckled again, shaking his head. "No worries. What I'm thinking is that if the systems in that place are still active, still powered up, we might need someone who can talk their language. Or who controls an AI that can talk their language."

Kayne thought for a moment. "You want me there so I can use QuIEK, if I have to."

"I'm something of a contingency planner," Kotler shrugged. "And I can see this contingency becoming something nasty.

The last thing I want is for us to be trapped in that place with no way out, thanks to some outdated computer system, or some nasty bit of tech we weren't aware of."

Kayne thought again and nodded. "Ok. Let me think about this."

"It's all I ask," Kotler nodded.

"So... you started this by asking what you could do for me," Kayne said.

Kotler arched his eyebrows. "You've thought of something?"

"I have," Kayne said. "The Decalogue stone..."

Kotler waited, then shook his head, his expression quizzical. "What about it?"

"I had QuIEK run it through a database of ancient languages. Best match was ancient Hebrew. And the translation... well, it was kind of... *familiar.*"

Kotler smiled. "The Ten Commandments," he said.

She shook her head. "Not exactly. I mean, yes, sort of. Close. But... how is that possible? How is there a stone with ancient Hebrew on it, in 1930s New Mexico?"

Kotler huffed, shaking his head. "Some people say it's a fake." He hesitated, looking at her on screen.

"Do you think it's fake?" Kayne asked.

Kotler hesitated a bit more, then shrugged. "I can't honestly say. I've never examined it directly, only from photos."

This didn't seem to satisfy her, and Kotler could see it by her expression.

He sighed again. "If you're asking me if I think there's the *possibility* of it being real... I'd have to say, yes."

This time it was Kayne's turn to arch her eyebrows. "Yes? Wow. So... how is that possible?"

Kotler leaned forward on his elbows. "There are a lot of strange bits of history in this region. A few years ago, I was part of a dig that revealed the presence of a Viking settlement in Pueblo, Colorado. I was also part of an exploration to retrieve an ancient plant from a cave in the Mojave Desert—a cave filled with Greek artifacts and writing. And I've personally explored a Celtic god's tomb in Egypt, where it definitely does not belong. The world is filled with out-of-place history."

"Sounds like you tend to find a lot of it," Kayne said.

"Seems that way," Kotler nodded, smiling.

She thought for a moment more. "I was brought into this because of a single phrase in the text message—*quantum encrypt*. So far, I haven't found any sign of anything that resembles quantum encryption."

"Maybe it's something Dr. Rivers found when she uncovered the Pit," Kotler replied.

Kayne nodded. "Maybe. Which sounds like a good enough reason for me to tag along, if I can."

"Couldn't agree more," Kotler replied.

"Good. But that really only leaves one big question mark, and it's the oddest one."

"The man with the face tattoo," Kotler nodded.

"What do you think that's about?" Kayne asked.

Kotler shook his head. "No idea. But sounds like the kind of thing that could lead to trouble."

Kayne laughed, shaking her head. "Judging from the expression on your face, it seems like trouble might be the most attractive part of this for you."

Kotler's expression was wry and knowing. "You too, I'm betting."

She smiled, shook her head, and sighed. "It was nice to meet you, Dr. Kotler. I'll be in touch."

"Wait!" He tried to stop her before she clicked off, but it was too late. The screen went dark, and the page Kotler had surfed to refreshed. Now it displayed a "404 Not Found" message, indicating that no such website existed. The URL was a dud.

Kotler sat back, shaking his head.

The things Alex Kayne could do. They were *astounding*.

It was no wonder the government was after her. She was genuinely *good* at this.

Which, of course, made her genuinely dangerous.

He turned his iPad face down, and stood to open the curtains, leaving the white noise to run. His hotel room gave him a view of the distant mountains, and the lights of Los Lunas.

The town was small, and a bit dreary, but it was Kotler's experience that towns like this held a lot more intrigue than one would expect.

Night had fallen on Los Lunas. Darkness had descended. Somewhere out there, an agent from Historic Crimes was in trouble. And it looked like Kotler and the rest of the team would be descending into something mysterious and danger-ous, in an effort to find her.

Kotler wasn't sure if Kayne was onboard or not, but he found himself hoping she was.

His gut was telling him that they might just need her.

CHAPTER THREE

DEEP UNDER THE MOUNTAIN, the man with the face tattoo—the one some called "the Comrade"—moved like silence itself.

He had long ago become accustomed to the darkness—not as complete as it might seem to one coming in from the surface world. To the Comrade, it was radiant. It was a world of vivid detail, shadows within shadows. Home.

The Comrade rarely visited the surface world.

He didn't find it appealing. Too much noise. Too much motion. Too many people, with their dramas and stories and relationships. The longer he lived in his underground domain, the more he found that the surface world was less and less necessary.

Here, in the silent dark, was good enough. It was everything.

He had food. Food for a millennium, under the right circumstances. Certainly enough food for his lifetime. Many lifetimes.

He had water. It flowed from an underground source, filtered through miles of rock, and then filtered again through an acre of algae followed by a network of carbon-filtered PVC channels. The carbon filters had to be changed once per month —a task that took him the better part of a day, working by himself. But changing them was as simple as removing the old filter and putting in the new one. The old filter was then placed in an oven, baked until it was clean of bacteria and debris again, and then re-shelved, waiting to be the next round of filter once again.

The Comrade had clothing, and blankets, and artificial sunlight. He had music. He had photographs. He had miles and miles of corridors to wander and more rooms to spend time in than he could get to in a dozen lifetimes.

He had practically everything he could ever need or want, here in the Pit.

What he lacked was books.

He had a lot of books, but not nearly enough. Not at the rate he consumed them.

When he'd first come to the Pit, he'd found the modest little library tucked into a wing of the third level. It had almost seemed quaint, considering that the US military had thought this would be enough books to keep an entire base mentally occupied for the duration of some decades-long experiment.

The Comrade had plowed through the entire library in less than three months, even with taking time away from reading to do routine maintenance on the Pit. Or to engage in... other tasks.

Now that he had things more or less running on autopilot, his leisure time had increased exponentially, but his supply of books had dwindled just as much.

And so he found, to his dismay, that he had to make trips away from the Pit. He had to go into Los Lunas, and sometimes further out, to bigger towns with more people. Sometimes as far as Albuquerque.

He dreaded those trips the most, avoided them for as long as he could stand to go without new books. And then, inevitably, he went.

Towns were challenging. He had no money—none other than what he could find and take, from time to time.

Money confused him, at any rate. He'd done things without it for so long, it was nearly a mystery to him how it all worked. He hated the whole idea of it—the capitalistic greed, the consumption mentality. He hated that there was a price tag on the things he needed. Why should anyone *pay* for what they *needed?* It was barbaric. It was disgusting. It was *America.*

Even with money in his pocket, he would steal. Simply take the books he wanted, a couple at a time, from grocery stores and drug stores and libraries. No one paid much attention at the libraries, but if he went there too often, he'd be recognized. So he had to be careful. Had to do things in a measured way.

He would sneak as many books as he could find into the aging pickup truck, fueled by gas siphoned from locals, and then drive home with his bounty. He'd arrive back at the Pit with crates of books, pilfered from dozens of locations, two or three per trip. He'd tote them in from the surface, crate by crate, and leave them on the floor until they could be shelved.

When the work was done, he'd drive the pickup into the tunnel, pull the doors closed, double-check the chains and locks and mesh fencing. And when he was satisfied that the Pit was secure again, he'd eagerly make his way to his new stash. He'd read them all within a few months, and would have to make the whole trip again.

This was how his collection had grown.

The modest library occupying one wing of the third level was now the *entire* third level. Soon it would spill over into level 4. At that point, the man might consider re-reading. At that point he would, by his count, have more books than even the big public library in Albuquerque had on its shelves. Surely that was enough?

Though, he had to admit, he would likely still make book runs until there was no more space on level 4.

After all, it was all living quarters on that level. He had his own quarters on level 4, and he didn't need much space. There were plenty of empty rooms, waiting to be filled. And it wasn't like he was going to have guests.

Not until recently.

The Comrade was content with the Pit. It was the perfect home, the perfect hiding place. And it was all his. No one else even knew it existed. He'd made sure of it.

He'd found the Pit while doing research, working a government job that made him sick—long hours, little pay, and dealing with the public the whole damned time. Disgusting. Horrific. Untenable.

He hated it. *Hated* it.

Hated it so much that he'd turned on the government itself. Turned on the whole *idea* of *America*. He embraced a different idea, a better idea. An idea that had gotten him a lot of nasty comments and people just flat out torturing him, day to day.

He took it. Embraced it.

The torture simply fueled his hate for the world he lived in, and extended that hate from America to its people, and then just to people in general.

People could all go to hell.

He would go to the Pit.

He'd first come across a reference to it while doing a property records search for a boisterous, annoying Texas billionaire —a man wearing a cowboy hat so big and so clean, he seemed like a parody. But he was dead serious about wanting to stake his claim on a piece of property in the hills of Los Lunas. He wanted to know who owned it, and how much they wanted for it.

Because to the man in the cowboy hat, everything was for sale.

And this patch of land was, too, as it turned out. But Comrade had no intention of revealing that. He'd decided it was a secret worth keeping. A secret that *had* to be kept.

Because in his searching, the Comrade had uncovered records of a government-run facility in the region—a place that was no longer technically in use, but was still on the government's books, albeit not something anyone bothered to elaborate on much.

The things the Comrade learned should not have been his to learn. They were secrets he should not have been privy to.

The Pit.

The name was given to the facility by a bunch of soldiers who had worked there for a time, men who had hated having to guard the place. Had, in fact, hated everything about it.

"A hole in the ground," one soldier said of it, in a letter to his superiors. The letter had been included as part of an official reprimand, after the soldier had gone AWOL for a weekend, turning up drunk and arrested in Albuquerque.

"Middle of nowhere" was another phrase. "No one for miles."

The Comrade had been intrigued.

The Pit was so secret, the government itself seemed to have forgotten about it. Every file was marked "eyes only." Every document was stamped "for redaction." Every scrap of paper on the subject of the Pit was something meant to be a buried secret.

The Comrade realized that none of the records he had in his possession should have *existed*. And yet, here they were.

And they told the Comrade *everything*.

The Pit had been decommissioned in the 90s, the research had been sealed, and the entire facility had been boarded up. All personnel were carted way, moved out of town, reassigned to new roles, their homes and possessions sold or simply abandoned.

Everyone who knew anything about the Pit was brushed away like crumbs from a table cloth.

The Pit was supposed to be an off-book, black operation. No records. Nothing official, nothing that wasn't redacted to the point of looking like a photo of midnight.

And yet, the Comrade had found records of it, anyway.

Someone had screwed up. Someone had filed public papers about a dark op facility. Someone had left a door open to the place—a portal to something rare and wonderful.

The Comrade recognized a rare opportunity when he saw one, and no one—especially not a blowhard in an oversized cowboy hat—was going to rob him of it.

He had walked out of his office and driven to the site that very day. Arriving as evening settled on the area, he had climbed out of his already aging pickup, and had used a flashlight to explore as much as possible.

It had taken some time, but he had managed to find a way in—a door that wasn't locked or covered with half a mountain of blown rock.

His entrance was a service garage, hidden on the far side of the hills from the main entrance to the Pit. It had been covered in brush and dirt and stone, most of it placed there deliberately, but with just a bit of effort the Comrade had unearthed it, and discovered that there was a hangar-sized garage on the other side of a large set of swing-out doors. Peering through the doors revealed a space where he could pull his truck inside, which he'd promptly done.

And then he'd gone exploring.

For a top secret, formerly secure government facility, it had been surprisingly easy to get inside. Basically, someone had left the back door open. And as the man explored, he discovered there was a lot more left behind as well.

The place was a treasure trove.

Everywhere the man went there were computers and offices and sleeping quarters. There were tools of every description in the garage, and throughout the complex there was equipment he couldn't even being to fathom.

Clothing, personal affects, office supplies—an endless array of resources.

And then there were the stores of food, the water treatment facility, the whole damned bunker.

The perfect space.

The perfect home.

All he had to do was keep it hidden.

Which turned out to be his life's work.

Over the next few years, the man worked hard to erase the Pit from living memory. One computer at a time, one database at a time, one former occupant at a time—delete, delete, delete. He used his limited access to public records to find and destroy every public scrap of info, and he used that info to find every living soul who knew about the place.

He'd gone to them. He'd questioned them. He got answers from them.

He eliminated them.

The Comrade hadn't had much of a taste for killing at first, but it had grown on him. He'd gotten creative about it, which made it interesting and even fun. Finding new ways to protect the secret of the Pit, new ways for those who knew of it to die, was a hobby of sorts. It presented him with both intellectual and physical challenges.

It was *stimulating*.

For a time, he tried to make every death look like an accident, mostly to keep it covered up. But after a while he realized, no one was paying attention.

Sure, the police were always interested. Dead bodies were always a red flag. There were investigations. But none of it ever led back to the Comrade.

How could it?

The deaths were too disparate, too scattered, too seemingly random. There was frankly nothing to connect them to the Comrade. And certain nothing to connect them to the Pit—that classified piece of real estate that only the Comrade had access to, had records for.

Records went missing, destroyed so that *only* the man was left to know the secret. And, the Comrade knew, in government, if it wasn't on paper, it didn't exist. Erase it from the minds of those who experienced it, and it was truly gone.

Over time, and with a lot of blood, the Comrade had managed to create a blank spot where the Pit used to be.

He'd done it. The secret was now his.

His secret, and his alone.

And with this secret came *freedom*. Not the cloying, bigoted, disgusting "freedom" Americans liked to crow about— the sort of liberty that lets one class thrive while another starves. This was freedom as each man was meant to have it! Freedom from *others*.

The Comrade could disappear into this new home and never have to deal with people again.

Well, except for the book runs. Those meant going into town. If he could just be satisfied with the books he had, he could end those, close the doors of the Pit, and rest in peace there, five miles below the world, far from the interference of humanity.

Except, of course, for the damned *girl*.

He had been on one of his book runs when the girl found the place.

He still wasn't sure how, but she'd somehow managed to track the facility down. Worse, she'd managed to *unlock* the place, coming in through one of the front doors—the doors that the Comrade himself had been unable to open.

All these years, all the tries, all the hammering against the other doors, the man had never managed to get them open. He'd tried drilling, but that had gone nowhere fast. He'd even tried ramming his truck into one set, resulting only in losing the front bumper. Those doors—those thick, impossible doors— they could never, ever be opened. Which, as he eventually realized, was perfect.

And yet here came the girl, waltzing into his home, right through those thick doors, like it was nothing.

When he had returned from his book run, he'd known right away that someone was in the Pit. He saw the marks, the evidence, the trail. He saw her car, parked down by the hill, and had covered that. But it was here, inside the Pit, that her presence was easiest to detect.

He could somehow sense her in there—he could practically *smell* her. The scent of body soap and perfume, of laundry detergent and fabric softener. The scent of *outside*.

It was the scent that drove him to hunt her.

He didn't like strangers in his home. Over the years, the decades, there had only been a few—perhaps less than five. They'd usually come in the same way he did, through the back door, in through the hangar.

He didn't know how many. He'd forgotten. Their deaths blended with other deaths, and he hadn't kept records.

But it had been a very, very long time, he knew that much.

He disliked strangers and worked hard to keep the Pit as buried as any place could be. So when he learned that the girl was here, when he *smelled* her, his first instinct was to find her, to kill her, and to turn her into food for his food. Fertilizer for his crops. Slice her up—he had a special tool for it. Grind her up. Spread her in the algae fields. Her rot would add nutrients to the garden.

There were many others there to keep her company, spread like fine soil, their blood feeding the algae, their flesh become his own food. Sometimes without the wait for decomposition.

Meat was meat.

But the smell of her.

The smell drove him to distraction. It filled him with something—a sensation within that he hadn't experienced in *so very long*. A yearning for something he couldn't even name. Something he'd given up on, even before he'd come to the Pit.

The smell reminded him of something lost, forbidden, cursed. Something that had driven a stake into him, brought bitterness into his life, caused him hurt beyond comprehension, and yet...

It was something he *wanted*.

Want and desire were emotions left behind for the Comrade, long ago. They held nothing good for him. Promises were always broken. And for years now, he'd wanted for nothing, and didn't miss the experience.

But now, here, in his own home, was a thing that stirred a long-lost urge within him—*desire*.

He didn't fully know what he wanted to do to her, but now that it burned inside him, he couldn't resist it. The one use he had for another human being, beyond food, beyond prey. The one thing any of them was good for.

He hunted her.

He tracked her through the levels—down, down, down.

She must have been here almost since the moment he'd left for the book run, because she'd gone *deep* into the Pit. She'd gotten further than any other stranger before her. She'd gotten to the levels even he was hesitant to enter. The places where things were strange, where the technology was incomprehensible, where the darkness was nearly complete.

The levels where the men who came before had done their darkest work.

She had some courage, and the Comrade liked that. It made things sweeter.

She was deep inside the Pit, and she'd been messing with the machines, with the computers. She'd done something. The Comrade wasn't sure what.

When he'd found her, she'd screamed. She'd fought him. She'd managed to get the upper hand, and to run.

She had made her way into the sixth level, where there were stores of food and water—the spaces that he'd converted into a larder, attaching shelves to the walls, stocking them with a backup supply of food, gathered from his runs into town. Food and goods beyond the stores of rations and MREs that had been stocked throughout the facility.

Not all the man's supply—but enough there to keep someone alive indefinitely.

The girl had locked herself into one of the storehouses next to an observation room, one that he'd never been able to break into in all the years. He'd tried. He'd attempted to smash the window, with no success. He suspected that it could take a bullet or a bomb if it needed to. This room was a place where something dangerous happened, observed by someone on the other side of the glass. It was a place where someone could hide out indefinitely. With all that food and water, the girl could survive in there for a very long time.

A permanent guest.

The Comrade wasn't sure if he could find a way in, but he would try. He would work it out, eventually, even if it meant scraping his way through the thick steel door. His sickle—the makeshift weapon he favored like an old friend, would get its taste.

But not before he did.

He had all the time in the world.

The girl wasn't going anywhere.

CHAPTER FOUR

"THIS IS NEVER GOING TO WORK," Kayne said, keeping her voice low.

She kept glancing around, fidgeting with the collar of her blouse, spinning the silver ring on her finger, trying not to seem too obvious but still feeling like there was a spotlight on her.

There were no spotlights. But there were agents. *Agents everywhere.*

Every instinct was telling her to run. After more than two years of listening to that instinct, she was finding it very difficult to ignore. But she managed to hold her ground, to keep trying for a casual look, to keep her screaming nerves in check.

Dr. Dan Kotler stood next to her, close by, apparently trying to be reassuring, though Kayne felt anything but reassured.

"You look completely different from the last time I saw you," Kotler said quietly, leaning in slightly.

He was *smiling*. That was annoying—it was like a touch of smugness, an over-familiarity that Kayne resented a bit. She wasn't sure why. Kotler seemed like a nice enough guy, but at the moment he was annoying the hell out of her.

Why isn't he freaking out, too? she thought.

The answer, of course, was that *he* wasn't on the FBI's top ten list, standing within cuffing distance of two armed agents.

She tried to calm herself, taking a couple of deep breaths, in through her nose, out through her mouth.

He was right, of course.

When she'd done the video chat with Kotler, a couple of days earlier, Kayne had been a brunette. Now she was sporting a dirty-blonde look that did a lot to change her general appearance. But there were other differences, as well. She had a bag of tricks, and she was pulling most of them out now.

"This isn't going to fool Agent Symon or Agent Mayher," Kayne said tersely.

Kotler nodded, then shrugged. "Doesn't have to. The two of them have been assigned duty in town, interviewing a few people, tracking leads. That sort of thing. They won't be accompanying us on this excursion."

That did make her feel a little better.

But only a little.

One of the two agents approached them and Kayne tensed, ready to bolt if she had to.

In her typical fit of over-prepared paranoia, she had arranged several escape routes from here—just in case. She could be out of here faster than anyone could say "zip line," in the wind and never to be seen by Kotler and his people again. She was always ready.

But if she and the agents moved from this location—which was the plan—her options would quickly become limited.

The agent—a man who looked like he'd likely been a quarterback at some point in his life—squared off with Kotler and Kayne, glanced at her, and then directed his comments to

Kotler. "We have coordinates for two entrances, thanks to the intel from Agent Symon's CI. We're rolling out in ten."

Kotler again nodded, then gestured toward Kayne.

Oh, I really wish you wouldn't...

"Roland, this is Dr. Alicia Carter. Liz assigned her to this. She's a new addition to the Computer Forensics team, a civilian specializing in encryption and decryption. She'll be our expert on whatever Dr. Rivers meant by 'quantum encrypt.'" Kotler smiled and turned to Kayne.

The agent reached out a hand, "Agent Roland Denzel, FBI. Well... I guess now it's FBI by way of Historic Crimes. I'm still getting used to it."

The agent smiled—a genuine and polite smile that did a lot to knock some of the edge off of Kayne's mounting paranoia.

She took his hand, "Same here," she said, and meant it. She was still getting used to the shift in her status with the FBI, from purely being a wanted fugitive to being... well, still a wanted fugitive, but also a CI. It was dizzying to consider what it all meant, or might mean.

"It's a pleasure to meet you, Agent Denzel," Kayne said, putting on a smile. "I've heard a lot about you." *From your file, and the deep background check I ran on you, and about a hundred news stories spanning the time since you hooked up with Kotler.*

Denzel shook her hand once, firm and assuring, then let it go. "Pleasure to meet you," he said.

She waited. But if Denzel recognized her, or had any hint of who she really was, he wasn't showing it.

She felt like sighing in relief, but held that in check.

Denzel turned back to Kotler. "You need anything, before we get on the road?"

Kotler shrugged. "Miracles and good fortune wouldn't hurt. But I'd settle for a cup of coffee."

Denzel scoffed and turned, leaving them standing there.

Kayne let out a breath she hadn't realized she'd been holding.

"I would really like to *not* do that again," she said.

Kotler laughed lightly. "Relax. Roland is a good guy. And he's used to working at the outer edges, mostly thanks to me."

She glanced around, then leaned in a bit to whisper, "You're not a fugitive. I *am*. And I've read up on Agent Denzel. He's as straight laced they come, just like Eric—*Agent Symon*." She shook her head, a quick gesture. "He'll arrest me, the second he figures out who I am."

Kotler sighed, then nodded. "Yes, he will," Kotler said. "But I've read *your* file, too. You're good at this. A master of disguise, quick on your feet. You probably have six different ways to get out of here, if things go sideways."

"Nine," she said, folding her arms over her chest.

Kotler laughed. "See? I don't think you have anything to worry about. You look nothing like yourself. Nothing like any photos I've seen of you, anyway. And certainly nothing like you did in our video chat."

This was true.

For the Alicia Carter persona, Kayne had gone to extra care to change her appearance entirely. She couldn't rely on prosthetics or anything that might come undone with time, but she'd taught herself a bunch of makeup tricks, thanks to YouTube tutorials. With the right application of eye liner, blush, and lipstick, she could virtually change the shape of her face.

It was an illusion, but it worked very well. She had breezed right by people who had memorized her features right down to her cheekbones, without so much as a blink.

For this gig, she had used makeup to give her face a fuller, more plump look, adding shadows and lines so she might appear a few pounds heavier. For good measure, she'd also plumped her figure up a bit. Shoulder pads, lifts in her shoes, a bit of padding in strategic places, and she appeared to be a woman about ten years older and twenty pounds heavier.

And she'd gone from brunette to blond.

She had opted not to wear a wig. Too easy to spot. But she had paid a special visit to a hair stylist operating out of her home in Los Lunas. Her request for "dirty blonde, as if the dye job is starting to wear off" had been unusual, but the Hispanic woman doing the coloring had seen, heard, and done stranger things in her time. And after nearly two hours of work, Kayne had paid the woman twice her usual rate, all in cash, and left looking very different from when she'd arrived.

She currently looked like a soccer mom turned computer forensics agent, which was precisely the look she was going for.

It was an impressive transformation. Enough to fool nearly anyone. But it didn't keep her from worrying that things could go South any minute.

She'd been recognized while in disguise before—the FBI and other law enforcement agents were trained to do just that, spotting fugitives in disguise. But her hope was that here, in the lion's den as it were, no one would be expecting her to pop up. Everyone would be so focused on finding Dr. Rivers that, she hoped, no one would pay attention to her.

That was the idea, anyway.

It helped a lot that Agent Symon wasn't here. She felt certain he'd recognize her instantly. No one knew her the way he did.

Thank God he was off site.

"Dr. Carter?" Kotler said. He had moved away, toward one of the off-road vehicles that would take them into the mountains. He had opened the rear door and motioned for her to climb inside.

She smiled. *Everything's fine*, she projected. *Nothing unusual here. No fugitives with advanced AIs in our presence. No need for handcuffs or throwing anyone into a cell.*

She climbed into the 4x4 and slid over to allow Kotler to slip in beside her.

"Down to three now," she said, quietly.

"Three?"

"Escape routes," she replied.

Kotler chuckled, and they fell silent as Agent Denzel and another agent climbed into the front seats, and the 4x4 lurched forward.

She'd been lying, of course. She had more than three escape routes. Just as she'd had more than nine while standing and chatting with Agent Roland Denzel.

One of the life lessons that her Papa Kayne had taught her now echoed in her head:

Never let them see all your cards.

It was good advice. It had saved her more than once. It was the reasons she always played with a loaded deck, making sure she had every contingency planned for, every door unlocked and every window left open. Papa's advice was the foundation of all of her golden rules.

Of course, she was actively ignoring another piece of advice that PaPa Kayne had always given her:

Never willingly climb into a car with trouble.

AGENT SYMON WAS GRUMPY.

This was clearly grunt work—driving all over Los Lunas, and out into the hills, asking questions of people who knew next to nothing about "the Pit," or Dr. Rivers, or anything else connected to this case. It was the sort of thing newbie agents were assigned to, when there was a team as big as this one.

Hundreds of agents from dozen of agencies, not to mention the civilians.

Symon was the top fugitive hunter in the *Bureau*. He was used to *running* operations like this one. Right now he felt like he had all the authority of a mailman.

He sighed.

Ego was something he actively tamped down in himself, but sometimes even he couldn't help it. He took a deep breath, letting it out slowly, and shook his head as he and Mayher approached the Los Lunas government records office.

The job isn't always glamorous, he reminded himself. *But you always do the job.*

They showed their badges at the front desk and explained why they were there, and the receptionist immediately ushered them into the office of the District Manager—a thin, balding man named Alfred Cox.

Cox seemed excited, even eager to speak with them.

"When the other agent came in, I knew something big must be happening!" His voice as a bit high pitched, and he exuded a sort of nervous excitement, like a chihuahua anticipating a trip outside.

"Other agent," Symon noted. "You're referring to Dr. Rivers?"

Cox nodded enthusiastically. "She was here about a week ago, I think. Came in looking for any records we had on a defunct facility North of here. We didn't have much—nothing at all, really. Just some survey maps and some stuff about the stone."

"Stone?" Mayher asked.

He grinned. "The Mystery Stone! It's famous. Most famous thing around here, anyway. See, it was written by the Egyptians, five thousand years ago, when they were living here with their gods."

He said all this in a knowing, conspiratorial tone, leaning forward, grinning.

Symon exchanged a glance with Mayher, then turned back to Cox. "I... thought the language was Hebraic?"

"Exactly!" Cox said, leaning back and slapping his desk with both hands, a satisfied look on his face. "It all comes together, see? The Hebrews were enslaved in Egypt. So the Egyptians took them out with them to find new lands to conquer," he waved vaguely toward some distant horizon. "Sailed in big Egyptian ships, and found America by accident, just like Columbus! And the Hebrews that came here with them carved that stone in secret. Kind of a quiet defiance, you know?" He was grinning absurdly, proud of his knowledge of ancient, alternate history.

Mayher frowned. "But... didn't the Hebrews get the Ten Commandments *after* they were liberated from the Egyptians?"

Cox again laughed and again slapped the desk. "Mysteries of history, am I right?"

Mayher looked again to Symon, who could offer no help.

"Mr. Cox," Symon said, leaning forward. "You mentioned that Dr. Rivers asked after a closed government facility?"

Cox nodded. "Sure, sure. We gave her everything we had. Land surveys, any records that might have something to do with it. Not a lot. We have a lot more about the stone, honestly. And that's what I told Dr. Rivers. She said she'd heard of the stone and thought it was interesting. But she was after the facility. I gave her everything we had, but I told her... I *told* her... you go look for that stone! That Mystery Stone holds *all* the answers!"

Symon wasn't sure what to say to this, but at the man's urging wave he glanced down to the notepad in his lap and jotted something there. *Mystery stone,* he wrote. It was the only thing he could think of.

"So," Mayher said, leaning forward, "did Dr. Rivers say where she was going after this? Did she happen to mention to you where she was staying?"

Cox thought, then shook his head. "Only thing I knew was that she was going into the hills, to find the stone."

"She actually went to the Decalogue stone?" Mayer asked.

"Oh yes," Cox said, his tone turning mysterious. "Sooner or later, everyone goes to the stone."

Mayher blinked, then jotted something in her own notebook.

"Mr. Cox," Symon said, "do you have copies of the records you shared with Dr. Rivers?"

Cox grinned, beaming, then stood and motioned for them to follow him. He led the two of them through the offices to a records room, a claustrophobic space crammed with lateral file cabinets from floor to ceiling. Cox hurried to one dark corner and rolled a ladder into place so he could climb and reach one of the higher drawers. He opened this, and practically dove into it, leaning forward and digging through the files.

"We keep meticulous records," Cox said as he shuffled down the ladder and handed a file to Symon. "That's why we don't allow anyone to remove the originals. I gave Dr. Rivers copies. You can have some, too, of course."

"We'll take it," Symon said, smiling at the man. "This is what you gave to Dr. Rivers? This is all of it?"

Cox's expression suddenly changed, becoming pained, and he nodded his head. "Yes, unfortunately. The rest has gone missing."

"Missing?" Mayher asked. "Stolen?"

Cox nodded again. "And I know exactly who took it. Andrew Jesup. The *Comrade.*"

Mayher and Symon exchanged glances, and Mayher asked, "Comrade?"

Cox nodded and sighed. "Worked here years ago. Not even sure how long. I was just a part timer then, but I remember him. Kind of leaves an impression. He went all anti-government, became a..." Cox stopped, looking from agent to agent, then around the room as if trying to make sure no one was listening. He leaned closer and said in a stage whisper, "Became a *commie*." He leaned back, shaking his head. "Took it to extremes, too."

"How so?" Symon asked.

Cox laughed. "Well, he went and got a face tattoo! Got the Soviet symbol inked right on his forehead, can you believe it?"

"Face tattoo..." Mayher said. She looked to Symon.

Symon said, "Soviet... as in the sickle and hammer? From the Soviet flag?"

"Exactly," Cox said, shaking his head. "He got real weird after that, started saying all kinds of crazy, anti-American stuff. Everyone just kind of tolerated him—he was doing his job, you know? Nobody liked him, but there wasn't much ground to fire him. Not until he started stealing."

"He stole records?" Mayher asked.

"I think so," Cox nodded. "But that wasn't what got him fired. He started stealing things from around the office. Toilet paper from the bathrooms. Food out of the fridge. Stuff like that. Last straw was when he got caught siphoning gas out of the cars in the parking lot. He disappeared after that. None of us were all that broken up about it."

Cox shook his head, then seemed to suddenly have a thought. "Hey! Do you want any of the records on the Mystery Stone? I gave them to Dr. Rivers, to take with her. I got tons of the stuff, mostly in my office. It's not official government info, really, but I keep one of the finest collections of records on the stone that there is."

He said this last with such pride that Symon and Mayher felt obliged to take copies of whatever he wanted them to have. He led them back to his office, where he used a copier in the corner to duplicate everything they'd brought from the records room, plus stacks and stacks of information about the Decalogue stone.

Nearly two hours had gone by since they'd arrived at the offices, and as they left, they loaded stacks of bundled papers into the back seat of their car. They drove away with Cox standing in the doorway, waving farewell after them.

"I'm not even sure what just happened," Mayher said.

Symon shook his head. "Me neither. But I think we have a lead to follow."

"Andrew Jesup?"

"Has to be 'the man with the face tattoo,' don't you think?" Symon asked.

Mayher had taken out her phone and was tapping something onto the screen. After a moment she replied, "I only show one Andrew Jesup in the state. Went missing nearly twenty-five years ago. Police report says the guy's landlord filed the missing persons report. Jesup hadn't paid rent in three months, and when the landlord opened the apartment, it looked ransacked. Furniture was still there, but the cabinets and drawers were all opened and emptied. It looked like someone might have robbed the place."

"And Jesup was never heard from again," Symon said.

"Looks that way," Mayher replied.

Symon huffed. "Ok. Let Agent Denzel know we have a lead, tell him we're going to start digging on this."

She nodded and made the call.

Symon pulled into a gas station to fill the tank, and while

he was waiting, he picked up the top sheet from the copies Cox had made for them. It was one of the Decalogue Stone records.

The sheet had a grainy black-and-white photo of the stone, with the carved characters highlighted. Beneath the photo there was a typed summary of what Frank Hibben—the archaeologist who had discovered the stone—insisted would be the meaning of the discovery.

Symon had seen Alex Kayne's translation of the stone. He didn't see how any of it related to Dr. Rivers' disappearance. But at this point, nothing could be ruled out. She *had* mentioned the stone in her text. So there was a connection.

The pump shut off, and Symon replaced the nozzle. He climbed back into the driver's seat.

"Got an address on the landlord. He's still alive. Lives in a senior care facility near here."

Symon nodded, and they started driving.

Thoughts of the Mystery Stone, and what it had to do with Dr. Rivers' disappearance, danced around in his mind. Along with those were thoughts of Alex Kayne.

He should check in with her soon.

Knowing her, though, she was at least a thousand miles away, staying off the radar as much as possible while helping out whoever her next client was.

Symon sighed.

He realized that if she were here, he'd have to arrest her. Deal or no deal, confidential informant or not, arresting Alex Kayne was his duty. He'd do it.

He sighed again.

Stay as far away from here as possible, he thought.

CHAPTER FIVE

THE DARK WAS STARTING to get to her.

Clara had been hunkered here for who knew how long—the darkness pressing in all around her, like a weight. Like the five miles of stone above her.

She could feel every mile, pressing, crushing.

The little bouncing digital clock on the computer next door had stopped being a comfort to her long ago, if it ever had been.

The silence was the worst of it. It scared her in a way she had never expected. She'd never heard such complete, utter silence in her life. It frightened her to every corner of her soul.

But it was the little things that broke the silence that frightened her more.

Skitters, somewhere in the darkness. The sound of something falling to the floor. The creak of something she couldn't identify.

The scraping.

It had started a few days ago, and at first she'd thought it was nothing. Just more of the Pit's quirks, she told herself. This was when she was still trying to be positive, still trying to keep herself together.

Scraaaaaaape.

It had come like a long sigh, from some unseen ghoul in the darkness. She couldn't quite figure out where it had originated, at first. It wouldn't matter if she could.

Some time later—she had no idea how long...

Scraaaaaaaape.

This time she'd been leaning against the door when it came, and she could hear that it was coming from the other side.

She wailed, but clamped her hand over her mouth, crab-crawling backward into the dark, toward the glass window that kept her from the only source of light she had, toward the bouncing clock on the computer display.

The sound didn't immediately come again.

Is he screwing with me?

The man with the face tattoo—that *stupid* face tattoo—had chased her to this room. He'd been screaming at her the whole way. "Get out! Get out! You don't belong here!"

She might have talked to him, might have reasoned with him, if it hadn't been for the thing in his hand. She didn't know what it was—a long, wicked hunk of metal, a jagged, broken end that came to a curved point. Maybe it was a broken machete. She wasn't sure. But it was clear that whatever it might once have been, now it was a weapon—a thing meant to rend and tear at flesh.

Like the man himself, it was something that seemed monstrous. Just its existence was revolting.

In her brief glimpse of it, she'd seen that jagged, hooked end and thought it was covered in dried blood. It was probably rust, she decided later. The thought that it was blood was just *too much*. She couldn't bare it, cringing here in the dark, thinking of that... that *thing*, drenched in blood and thirsty for more.

Thirsty for *her* blood.

She wouldn't allow herself to even think about it.

She'd given the man the slip for a while, ducking into corridors and rooms. She'd come across a vast space filled with pools—like below-ground swimming pools, but filled with something green and gross. Algae, maybe? It was in that room that she'd dropped the phone into the drain. The only thing she could think to do.

It seemed so stupid now.

She'd give anything to have that phone back. That light. No signal, sure, but she'd at least have *light*. Photos to look at. Music to listen to. *Something* to remind her that there was a world outside this room, somewhere.

It would have been a huge comfort, until it died.

Why had she tossed it away? She wasn't even sure it would reach anywhere that had signal—it was just...

Scraaaaaaape.

She screamed, and again scurried backward, pushing herself into a rack of canned goods. Something fell on her from above, like a sandbag, and she thought her heart would explode.

She felt around for it.

A bag. Paper. Soft. Firm.

Flour, she thought.

She could feel that some of it had leaked out on her. She could feel the silty grains of it on her face, her shoulders, in her hair. She was probably covered in the stuff.

Flour gets everywhere, she thought. *It gets everywhere...*

She remembered the first and last time she'd tried baking. Dropping the bag of flour. The explosion of it, settling over everything like dust. There was still flour on things when she moved to a new place, four years later.

She laughed at the memory, relieved for it.

But the sound scared her, in the silence of the room,

echoing from the walls, the glass of the window. It didn't sound natural. It sounded disconnected—*disembodied.*

She laughed again. This time, it sounded even worse. High pitched, panicked, *insane.*

She was going to go insane in this place.

She had to *get out of this place.*

Scraaaaaaape.

Another scream, and now she was crying, pulling her knees to her chest, burying her face against them, holding her hands to her ears.

Scraaaaaaaape.

She picked up the bag of flour and threw it at the door where it exploded in a puff of particles, erupting in all directions.

In the dim, green-tinted light from the computer's screen-saver, she could see a cloud of dust rise and shift, moving in the air of the room, like a phantom.

Her mind started making shapes of it, started finding patterns in it. A face—glowing green, shifting as if alive, two large, empty eyes, a gaping mouth, the clear expression of malice and hate and *hunger...*

Scraaaaaaaape.

Clara moaned and fought a scream as she scrambled to her feet, knocking more cans and other unseen objects from the rack behind her. She started frantically grabbing at everything she could put her hands on, reaching, pulling, finally climbing.

She found herself on the top of the rack, which was firmly bolted to the cinderblock wall. She reached the top. She pulled herself into a ball and sobbed.

She didn't know why she was up here. It just felt like the thing to do. Get as high off of the ground as she could. Get as far from the door as she could. Get away from the man—the *thing* outside the door.

Scraaaaaaape.

He was out there.

The man with the face tattoo was playing with her. *Trying* to scare her.

And it was working.

And that finally pissed her off.

The light from the screensaver wasn't much, but it was enough to light up the particles of flour, drifting in the air. She could still see them shifting and lingering, floating as motes in the tiny green light.

She had an idea.

She took a few deep breaths, let them out slowly, got herself as calm as she could manage.

Scraaaaaaape.

Nope, she thought. *Not this time.* She tightened her jaw, clenched her fists, took deep, calming breaths.

Though, in truth, her heart started racing again at the sound. Adrenalin was pumping through her. She was more scared than mad—but at least she was mad and getting madder.

And she would use it.

She was a scientist. She was a *federal agent*, for God's sake! This B-Movie horror crap wasn't going to take her down. Not without a fight.

She was still on the top shelf of the storage rack, but now she was looking down, assessing.

The particles of flour had started to settle back to the floor. The air was clearing. Only a few wafting clouds could be seen in the bouncing light of the computer display.

She climbed down to the floor, stepping carefully. She'd managed to make the space a minefield of tripping hazards, in her panic.

When she got to the door, she had to feel around for the bag of flour.

It had burst open, and was laying in a drift of its former contents, sagging like its life had been drained from it. A husk of its former self.

She felt for the mound of flour on the floor. She grasped some of it in her hand and then stood and faced the window.

The clock showed 2:45. It was about to bounce from one corner of the screen. Its greenish light seemed barely visible, though it was bright enough for what she had planned.

She held up her palm and blew on the little pile of flour there.

A tiny cloud puffed into the air, and she watched it. She focused every bit of attention she had on it. She strained eyes, following it.

Scraaaaaaaape.

Screw you!

The puff of flour rose and then moved.

It was hard—almost impossible—to see where it went in the dim, nearly invisible light from the screensaver. But it gave her the direction. She had a course to set.

She once again climbed the rack, but this time she was moving toward a goal. She had to shove more things off of the top shelf, as she went, and the clatter to the floor was nerve-wracking. Surely the man with the face tattoo could hear it, too. He had to be wondering at what she was doing. Would he figure it out? Would he be able to get to her, if she went through with this?

By the time she reached her destination, the adrenaline was making her shake and tremble.

Scraaaaaaaape.

It felt like a spike through her guts, but she didn't scream. She couldn't panic. Not now.

She reached out with her hand, felt along the wall.

There!

A grate.

Small, but not too small. She was slender. Yoga. Thank God for Yoga! She could fit.

She ran her fingers along its edges, searching.

Two screws.

That was it. Just two screws, and maybe—*maybe*—she had a way out!

She would find something in this room. She'd make a screwdriver, somehow. She could do that. She was clever, she reminded herself. She'd figure this out, and she'd get *out of here*.

The princess is saving herself in this one, she thought, and laughed.

She tried not to be bothered by the fact that the laugh sounded just as panicked as it had earlier. Any sound, *every* sound, was as awful as that scraping sound, in this darkness.

Scraaaaaaape.

She felt herself crying, almost sobbing, but couldn't quite decide what it meant. And it didn't matter. She had a job to do.

She got to work.

CHAPTER SIX

The drive into the hills surrounding Los Lunas was pretty uneventful, and Kotler was using the time to scan through some history surrounding the Decalogue stone, looking for anything that might provide some insight into how the stone was connected to Dr. Rivers and the Pit.

Kotler and Denzel had visited the stone on the day they'd arrived in New Mexico, hiking into the hills with a couple of local experts, inspecting the stone itself. Kotler had snapped several images using his phone, but they were no more revealing than anything he could have found online.

The site had been visited by thousands of people over the years, each leaving their own little trace of history here and there, in small and sometimes big ways. Tourists left finger-prints that inevitably changed the story of the stone, despite its remote location and the requirement of a permit to visit. After so many decades of this, it might be impossible to discover the truth about it.

Kotler had studied the stone from every angle, including all available translations. He added Alex Kayne's translation to the pile and was impressed at the thoroughness. There were cross references within cross references, and links to in-depth research into the stone. There was also a complete history—everything anyone anywhere knew about "The Los Lunas Mystery Stone," ranging from expert opinion to amateur speculation and conspiracy theories.

It was an incredible amount of information—there were entire academic journals that had fewer citations and references.

Unfortunately, it all added up to exactly nothing, as far as Kotler could determine. Nothing that would help with finding Dr. Rivers, at any rate.

He glanced up from his iPad, rubbing his eyes. He could hear music coming from the 4x4's stereo, and between that and the rumble of the engine, plus the wind and road noise as they crossed the rough terrain, it was difficult to hear the conversation that Denzel and the other agent were having.

He glanced to his side and noted that Alex Kayne was sitting nearly rigid, watching the landscape pass by.

He leaned toward her. "I was just looking over the files you sent to Agent Symon," he whispered.

She glanced quickly at the two FBI agents in the front seat, and Kotler shook his head. "Nothing to worry about."

"Says the one who *isn't* wanted by the *feds*!" Her voice was a fierce whisper, so quiet in comparison to the noise of the vehicle that Kotler almost couldn't hear her from just inches away.

He smiled and shook his head again. "I've had my turn at that. Though, admittedly, I wasn't a fugitive for anywhere near as long as you've been. I'd love to pick your brain about that some time."

Kayne frowned. "About being on the run? Why?"

Kotler shrugged. "I'm an anthropologist, and something of

an amateur psychologist. I like to know why people do the things they do. The best way to learn is to study the more... abnormal behavior."

He'd tried to choose his words carefully, but if Kayne was offended, she showed no sign.

"I do what I do because it keeps me from living the rest of my life in a cell," she said with a shrug.

Kotler laughed. "Oh, I think it's quite a bit more than that. I've seen your file. You could be anywhere on the planet right now. But you're here."

"Chalk it up to bad habit," she frowned.

"What's the habit?" Kotler asked.

Kayne sighed, shaking her head. "Something my grandfather taught me. Something that's more or less been my... I don't know, my guiding principle. *Always finish the job.*"

Kotler smirked, shaking his head again. "Ok, again, I'm pretty sure it's more than that. What makes you take on these jobs in the first place?" He held up a hand. "Actually, I think I know the answer to that."

She gave him a surprised look. "So what do you think it is?"

He shrugged. "It isn't a big mystery. You're on the receiving end of an injustice. A pretty big one. It's unfair, and it's upturned your whole life. There doesn't seem to be anyone you can turn to who can actually help. But you have something that gives you a kind of super power—QuIEK makes it easy for you to move around in the world, I'm guessing. And you're the type of person who feels responsible. So, you help people who don't have the advantages you have. People like you, who are being let down by the system. I think that instead of running, this is your way of fighting back."

She said nothing, but looked out the window for a moment. Finally she turned back to him. "So, you've been pretty focused on all that research about the stone. Found anything?"

He shook his head. "No. Nothing useful."

Kayne considered this and shook her head as well. "Me neither. I can tell you everything that's ever been put online about that stone, but I can't tell you how it connects with Dr. Rivers, or the Pit."

"But the Pit," Kotler said, suddenly warming up. "That's something! You managed to get a lot of details."

"Hardly anything, really," she said. "There's a lot missing."

Kotler was surprised. "There is? How do you know?"

She thought for a second, then scooted closer, leaning in. "Ok," she said, "so here's the thing. QuIEK is an AI. It's about as intelligent as a piece of software can get, but it's still dependent on input and instructions to know what to do, what to look for. I'm pretty good at feeding it the right input, asking the right questions. It's not as simple as asking it to 'go and fetch me X.' I have to point it in the right direction and ask for exactly what I want."

"Ok," Kotler nodded.

"I did that here. I've done it a million times. I get a lot of answers. A lot of data. And in all that, even though QuIEK is pulling it all together, applying logic, weeding things out, I still have to have a sense of what belongs and what doesn't. And... well, also what *isn't* there. I started picking up hints of that, while the data was coming in. Something is *missing*. Someone deleted records. Deliberately hid things. And..." She paused, glancing forward as Agent Denzel's phone rang, the ring tone audible even over the noise of the 4x4. He answered it and started talking in a low voice to whoever was on the other side.

"What is it?" Kotler asked.

Kayne shook her head. "It's more than just records," she said. "*People* have gone missing, too. People connected to this facility. To the Pit."

"Missing," Kotler replied.

"Some turned up dead," she said. "Lots of accidents. A few suspected murders. Some people were tortured. I don't think the police knew there was any connection, any kind of pattern to it. The Pit was an off-book project, top secret. There's no real way to know that a murder in Dallas might be connected to half a dozen other murders all over the country. So unless you happened to know that these people were all working together on a secret project—one that isn't even around anymore—you wouldn't necessarily see any connection."

"Disparate cases, with nothing to alert anyone that there's a link," Kotler nodded. "Ok, I can see the problem. But *you* found the link."

"QuIEK did. But yes, it's there. Someone has been covering this up. Someone doesn't want there to be any record of the Pit. And there isn't, as far as it goes. Public records are all scrubbed. Only the classified stuff is still out there. No one has access to it, really, unless they know it's there, and have the clearance to get to it."

"No one but you," Kotler smiled. "And QuIEK."

She nodded. "Right. For all the good it's done."

They bumped along the gravel road, letting the conversation fade as they contemplated what they knew and what it might mean.

Suddenly Denzel ended his call and turned in his seat.

"That was Agent Mayher," he said, raising his voice to be heard over the noise of the drive. "She says that she and Agent Symon are running down a lead. Guy's name is Andrew Jesup. He has an interesting face tattoo."

"Face tattoo?" Kotler asked. "That can't be a coincidence."

"Symon and Mayher don't think so," Denzel said. "Guy was a wannabe communist. He had a sickle and hammer tattooed on his face, maybe as some kind of statement. He worked in the local government records office, and they think he may have scrubbed the place of any information about the Pit, before he disappeared."

Kotler arched his eyebrows, then nodded. "Well, that tracks."

"It does?" Denzel asked.

Kotler could have kicked himself. He felt Kayne tense beside him.

"That someone local would have to have known about the Pit," Kotler said, recovering. "Dr. Rivers had to have found out about it somewhere."

Denzel considered this, then nodded, turning back in his seat and facing forward.

"Smooth," Kayne said, with a hint of smile in her voice.

"Maybe I need an AI to run my mouth," Kotler replied, settling back.

THEY RODE in quiet for several more miles, along a bumpy gravel road. The condition of the road was poor, with loose gravel and a fine, gritty sand heaped in mounds along previous tire tracks. It was clear that it hadn't seen much use in quite some time.

It was dangerous to drive more than ten or twenty miles per hour here, even in a four-wheel-drive. So the entire ride was a slow, tedious, jarring journey that left everyone feeling jangled and frazzled by the end of it.

As the 4x4 pulled to a stop, the agent in the driver seat—Agent Barr, Kayne had finally learned—turned to them and said, "At least we get to do that all over again on the way back."

There were courtesy laughs from Kotler and Denzel, but Kayne found herself wondering if anyone would notice if she hired a helicopter for a pickup.

"Ok, everyone out," Denzel said. "GPS says the entrance

we targeted is here, somewhere. Keep your eyes peeled. And no one goes in alone, got it?" He directed this last comment mostly toward Dr. Kotler, who smirked, shrugged, and nodded.

Kayne climbed out of the 4x4 and stood, stretching her aching back as she surveyed the hill before her.

This was, as officially as it could be, the middle of absolutely nowhere.

The facility she'd uncovered in her research had to be remote by its very nature. Isolation was key when you were doing strange and mysterious things that may or may not be strictly sanctioned by federal laws or international treaties. There hadn't been a lot of specific details about what went on here, but what few details Kayne had uncovered sounded like a season of *Black Mirror*.

She wasn't sure what she'd been expecting once they arrived. She knew there wouldn't exactly be signs and spotlights directing them in. Secret bases tended to be hidden. But here, standing in the hills outside Los Lunas, miles from anyone and anywhere, they appeared to just be nowhere at all.

She checked her phone and was relieved to see she had a signal. Weak and anemic, a single bar, but it was LTE. That was good. She could work with that.

She didn't necessarily need an internet connection to run QuIEK. Despite the power of the AI software, it was actually quite compact. She could run it entirely from her smartphone, and often did.

Connectivity was more of a security blanket. She had other resources—a virtual network of microcomputers she called Smoke Screen, hidden close to internet hotspots in cafes and hotels and bars across the country. If she had connectivity, she could reach out to these in a pinch. Extra processing power, not to mention the odd Google search, could always come in handy.

So it was a relief to see she was still online. At least out here, in the open.

She smiled, then laughed quietly.

Poor fugitive would miss her internet.

To be fair, over the past two years, as she'd been on the run, internet connectivity had become her lifeline to anything resembling a normal life. Where she had to remain fairly isolated, out here in the three-dimensional world, she could be anyone she wanted to be online. Anonymity was just part of the scene.

So the majority of her interaction with others was done online. Her community was there. It wasn't quite the same as being able to drop onto a padded chair in a Starbucks and reminisce with an old friend—in fact, she had to maintain a strict no-contact rule when it came to anyone in her old life. But she did have "friends" online. She'd managed to keep up relationships with a few souls here and there. Never family or friends from her past. Never even her former clients, except in extreme cases.

But she did have *some* human connection, even if they never knew who she really was.

She shook her head and moved forward, scouting the ridge line, looking for any sign of an entrance to a defunct, classified government facility.

When she reached the top of one mound of stone, she looked out over the expanse of hills and rocky terrain, stretching in every direction.

It really would be easy to disappear in a place like this, she thought. *Isolated. Secure. No one would ever find you.*

It had some limited appeal.

Kayne was not, by her nature, a recluse. She liked people. She liked them a lot. And that had been one of the roughest parts of being on the run. As a fugitive, keeping people in your life was a luxury you just couldn't afford.

So, for the past couple of years, she'd been a loner. She made contact with her clients—the people suffering injustice, ignored by law enforcement, needing her help. But that contact was short. Empty. No real connection.

Of course, there was Agent Symon.

One of the few people she communicated with regularly who actually knew who she was—just not *where* she was. Most of the time.

Symon had actually gotten closer to catching her than any other agent. He'd nearly had her, a couple of times. He'd *literally* put his hands on her, once, in Orlando. But in the end, even Agent Symon, the FBI's best fugitive hunter, was no match for Alex Kayne's hyper paranoia and obsessive planning. She'd managed to get away and stay away, and she'd been a few steps ahead of him ever since.

Since then, though, she'd formed a sort of relationship with him. Phone calls, video calls, text messages. Even the occasional face-to-face chat.

It was like dancing at arm's length, but it was the most *real* human contact she'd had in years.

Until today, anyway.

Kayne glanced back over her shoulder at the FBI agents and Dr. Kotler.

Dr. Dan Kotler—now he was something.

She wasn't entirely sure *what*, but *something*.

She'd never met anyone like him. Clearly very intelligent. Dry sense of humor. Always ready with a quip or a grin. And apparently always in a little trouble. She could relate.

But there was something else. Something only someone like Alex Kayne, fugitive and reluctant recluse, could pick up on.

Kotler was *running*.

Maybe not the same way Kayne was. No one seemed to be after him, trying to bring him down or lock him up. Not at the moment, anyway. But she couldn't shake the idea that Kotler was hiding behind his quirks and mannerisms, projecting something to the world that was more play than reality.

Dan Kotler was in *disguise*.

What he might be hiding, or hiding from, Kayne couldn't say. But a runner knows another runner, when she sees him. And Dr. Dan Kotler was a runner. Just like her.

It made him...

What, exactly?

Relatable. And, strangely, something of a comfort.

Kayne couldn't afford to blindly trust anyone, but she was having a hard time keeping her shields up when it came to Dan Kotler. He'd already gotten closer to her than anyone else—including Agent Symon. A single word from him, right this moment, would put her in handcuffs. She really should know better. She *did* know better.

And yet...

She was looking in the direction of Kotler and the two agents as they fanned out, searching, when she saw the glint of something not far from where the 4x4 was parked.

"Hey!" she shouted, pointing. "There's something there!"

The men turned, following where she pointed. She scrambled down the hillside and joined them as they pushed through some brush and up over a mound of loose stone.

Parked at the foot of a ridge, covered in branches and debris, was a sedan.

It was filthy, with dust caked on the windshield and in the wheel wells, covered in tumbleweeds and brush.

It was a miracle that it had made it here, over the rough terrain, with no four-wheel drive.

"Rental," Agent Barr said, pointing to a sticker on the back glass.

"Dr. Rivers' car," Denzel agreed, peering in the driver-side window. He stood, turning in a slow circle, looking at the landscape around them. "The entrance has to be close."

"So far I'm not seeing anything," Kotler said.

Agent Barr concurred.

Kayne, however, was thinking.

The text message that Rivers sent had several cryptic references. One of those—*quantum encrypt*—was the biggest reason Kayne was here.

It was a clue. And it tickled something in Kayne's brain.

So far they hadn't found anything to indicate what that reference meant, but Rivers had mentioned that the Decalogue translations plus quantum encryption had gotten her in—presumably "in" meant "into the Pit." So, it seemed likely that Rivers' had somehow opened the door using quantum encryption, and that the Decalogue stone was somehow part of that.

The stone was miles from where they stood. There was just no way it had any role in opening the door to this place. Not physically.

But the *information* from the stone was right in Kayne's pocket.

She turned her back to the agents and Dr. Kotler, and took out her phone. Using QuIEK, altering how the phone's radio antennas functioned, she started pinging any local signal she could find. She immediately picked up the bluetooth and wireless signals from the smartphones each man was carrying, plus the signal from Dr. Kotler's iPad, still in the 4x4.

But another signal was there as well. A strange one.

Strange, because it had the characteristics of a wireless data stream, but it was different from anything Kayne was used to.

Not a bluetooth signal. Not even cellular. Close, though. Something *related* to a cellular signal, like an early ancestor.

Kayne considered this.

This facility was abandoned in the 90s. Cellular technology was alive and well in that era. Wasn't it possible that there could be some sort of early LTE tech here?

Government and military technology tended to be about 20 to 30 years ahead of civilian tech, by most estimates. So it could be possible that there was technology here that had eventually been surpassed in the private sector. Old tech, but still part of the framework of modern cellular systems. A distant cousin. Or, more likely, an ancestor, generations older than modern-day LTE.

The protocol known as LTE—which stood for "Long Term Evolution"—had been proposed as a cellular phone standard in 2004, but its origins could be traced back to the late 80s. Early versions of the tech could have been in use by select entities, and entities rarely got more select than secret government facilities.

She had QuIEK connect to the signal, and start following it, tracing it back to its origin.

She came up against a firewall immediately, blocking all access.

And *that* was interesting.

Because QuIEK—the Quantum Integrated Encryption Key—simply did not *notice* firewalls. It was a digital skeleton key that could get her into any system, any time.

And it would get her into this one, too. It was already working its way around the roadblock, finding its weaknesses, negotiating with it to open the lock. QuIEK would get in.

It was just going to take longer than usual.

Because, she was stunned to discover, the "firewall" she'd bumped into was, itself, built on quantum encryption.

The implications of this were stunning. Quantum encryption, in the 90s? Who was working on anything like this, during that era? The idea had been around for a long time, since the early 80s at least, but technology built on the theories hadn't come along until the past twenty years or so. Kayne had been a part of the birth and evolution of that tech.

QuIEK was hardly the first quantum encryption software to exist—it just happened to be the best. There were others. But Kayne had rarely encountered anything as advanced as what she was seeing here.

The people who built this place, the things they were experimenting with—this was *big*. Change-the-world big. So what had caused them to shut it down?

And if *this* was the lock on the front door, what would they find inside?

She started working at the lock, using QuIEK to push at its edges. It was good, and under any other circumstances it would be unbreakable. But QuIEK was already making headway.

At this rate, she'd have it open in a couple of days.

Not quite good enough.

Was there a way to do this faster?

She was thinking this through when Kotler walked up to her.

"Hardly the time to check in on Twitter," he said, smiling.

She looked up, blinked, and gave a smile in return. "You're not going to believe this," she whispered. She walked him through what she'd found, and he stepped in beside her, peering at her phone's screen as QuIEK did its thing.

"It would help if I could figure out the encryption key for this," she said, shaking her head. "QuIEK will crack it, but it's going to take a few days. With the key, I could be through in seconds."

"So if you only had the password?" Kotler smiled.

She shook her head. "No, not the password. I mean, yes, if we had that, we'd be in. But this is different. The key is more like an address. Like GPS coordinates. A map of quantum states, basically. It would tell us exactly where to start, and more or less show us a roadmap of the security for this thing. A basic quantum decryption would be able to crack this in a few hours, with that key. Maybe a day. QuIEK would do it in seconds."

Kotler was staring at her.

"What is it?" Kayne asked.

"I'm thinking about the text message," he said. "*Decalogue translations plus quantum encrypt.*"

Kayne considered this.

"The Decalogue Stone," Kotler said.

Kayne blinked. "You think that's the encryption key?"

He shrugged. "You'll have to tell me."

She considered this, then pulled up the files she had on the stone. She had digital translations and scans. She fed these to QuIEK and had the AI start working on how they could be applied.

It took only a moment. QuIEK ran every permutation, finally settling on the symbols from the stone itself, translating them into a set of quantum coordinates based on their general shapes.

It was the sort of intuitive system that would have been out of reach for any other quantum encryption software, but QuIEK's advanced AI made short work of it.

Kayne and Kotler watched the phone's display as a string of Hebraic characters lined up, then disappeared, leaving behind a cascade of code that eventually resolved into something they could read.

Access Granted.

Kayne looked up at Kotler, who seemed as surprised and thrilled as she did.

"What did that just do?" Kotler asked.

Kayne was shaking her head, about to answer, when Agent Denzel yelled up at them.

"We got something!" he shouted. "A door just opened in the side of the rock! Get down here!"

Kayne and Kotler looked at each other, then scrambled down the hill to meet the other agents. In moments they were standing at the front door of the Pit, which stood wide open, a gaping hole in the mountainside.

"No welcome mat," Kotler said.

"If anything, it screams 'do not enter,'" said Agent Barr.

"Let's get it together," Denzel said. "Gear up. We're going in."

They pulled on gear, got themselves prepared.

And then they descended into the dark.

CHAPTER SEVEN

JESSUP—WHO by these days had been called *the Comrade* for so long, he could barely remember even *having* another name— stared at the door. He didn't like the sounds coming from the other side.

In his hands he held death. And she was beautiful. And she was necessary.

He couldn't allow visitors to just *leave* the Pit. They'd tell someone what they saw. They'd reveal this place to someone, and all the Comrade's work would be undone.

The weapon made easy work of most folks.

He called her *Móki*.

Móki was made from scrap he'd found on the site—a blade from the tail rotor of some long-gone helicopter. He'd come across it when he'd first explored the Pit, found it laying in a pile of scrap. It had met with something hard and immovable at some point, from the look of it, and its tip had snapped off. The stalk of the thing was still intact, and the Comrade had used a hacksaw to cut it down, then ground it with an angle grinder to get it into a decent shape for a handle.

The result was about a three-foot-long blade, straight as an arrow until it ended in that jagged curve. It looked a bit like the sickle he'd had tattooed to his face. It looked thirsty for the blood of intruders.

He loved it.

And he used Móki for all sorts of things in the Pit. He always had it with him, though he did stash it in the truck when he made his book runs. Móki was noticeable. She called attention to herself and to him. That wouldn't do, when trying to sneak books out of the library or bookstores or grocery stores. Attention was no good.

Regardless, Móki was always close by. And she had seen a lot of use, inside and outside the Pit, over the decades. She had tasted plenty of blood and left plenty of cold behind.

Right now he was dragging her sharpened tip along the surface of the door, the only barrier between him and the woman. He was letting the sound echo and hang in the darkness of the Pit, knowing that it would do some of his work for him.

Fear was a good tool. It made people panic, made them do things they shouldn't. If he couldn't quite break through the door physically, he could reach the woman with that sound. Móki's mewling for blood.

But on the other side of the door, there'd been a racket he wasn't expecting.

It sounded like the woman was throwing things off of the shelves in there. Making a mess. A mess he'd have to clean up once he was done with her.

If he was ever done with her.

He pulled the bladed down the surface of the door one last time.

Scraaaaaaaape.

And now he'd leave. He'd had enough. He needed to tend

to some things elsewhere. And the girl wasn't going anywhere. She might have locked him out, but he'd managed to lock her right back in.

Stalemate.

He tapped the tip of Móki on the door a few times, then turned and marched back down the corridor, letting the hook dangle at his side.

He needed to get the truck unloaded and then do his rounds.

The woman had gotten in here somehow, and he was going to figure out how, to make sure it didn't happen again.

He was just about to round a corner when he heard the voices.

He felt his heart pounding, from his chest and all the way up into his temples.

Did she bring people here?

It was his fear. The one thing that made him afraid. And angry.

He felt rage boiling. He felt the old call. He felt the weight of Móki in his hand, the press of it against his leg, the call for blood.

Slowly, quietly, he moved to the corner and peered around.

He could see their lights now—lanterns and flashlights, intruding on his precious darkness, hurting his eyes.

He ran a finger over the curved edge of Móki, felt the jagged sharpness of her, and smiled as it sliced the tip of his finger. Blood dripped onto the blade, then onto the floor.

His blood. The first feed.

The next feed would be fresh and new, and Móki was sure to love it.

· · ·

KOTLER WAS AHEAD of the others, using a flashlight to cast a wide circle ahead of him. This corridor was long, but there were many branches leading from it, deeper into the darkness of this place.

They'd ridden an elevator to get down this far—something Agent Denzel had barely tolerated, with his claustrophobia. Neither Agent Barr nor Alex Kayne knew about Denzel's phobia, but Kotler had watched his partner closely the whole ride down. Just being here, in the Pit, was putting a bit of strain on his friend. But he held up—he'd developed a few tricks, over the years. Some with Kotler's help. He was getting through it.

Still, Kotler was keeping an eye on his friend, just in case.

Right now, however, he had both eyes fixed on every detail of the corridor stretching before him.

Something had his intuition buzzing.

He was hard pressed to say what it was—maybe he'd caught some barely audible sound, or seen some tiny movement out of the corner of his eye. Or maybe he was just feeling the pressure of being five miles below the mountain.

That seemed unlikely, however.

Unlike Denzel, Kotler had no fear of tight spaces. He'd spent the better part of his adult life, and a bit of his boyhood, exploring and spelunking and occasionally getting trapped in everything from natural caverns to ancient tombs. He couldn't say he relished the experiences, exactly. But he did find the whole thing *familiar* at least.

So he doubted that he was having any anxiety about being trapped down here. It seemed more likely that he'd subconsciously picked up on some queue.

Maybe he'd caught a bit of Dr. Rivers' trail?

He glanced back down the corridor. True to his promise, he hadn't wandered far. The rest of the group was standing and chatting, considering options. Denzel and Barr were comparing notes, trying to work out their next steps, choose their next direction. Kayne stood off to the side, her back to the boys and her eyes glued to her phone.

Kotler knew she was doing something with QuIEK—but she looked for all the world like a sullen teenage girl just trying to get a signal so she could chat with her friends.

He smiled and chuckled... and then suddenly he was grabbed and thrown to the floor.

Kotler hit the concrete hard, but managed to get his hands under him. They smacked the concrete, jarring him and sending a wave of numbness up his right forearm.

The flashlight went spinning down the side passage as Kotler rolled quickly onto his back.

A man stood above him, disguised by the darkness until the rolling flashlight spun, casting a bright wash of light onto the man's whole form.

Kotler saw the face tattoo—the hammer and sickle.

He had just enough time to register what it was, *who* this was, before noticing the man was raising some sort of wicked looking blade above his head.

Kotler reacted, spinning on his back, kicking out his legs to entangle them with those of the man.

As the blade arched downward, Kotler rolled, catching the man's legs with his ankles. Kotler pulled his knees toward his chest, clipping the man in the back of his own knees and sending him sprawling to the ground.

He was close. Too close.

The man said nothing, made not even a grunt, but raised the curved blade once again.

Now, less than a foot from Kotler, there was no avoiding what was coming next.

The best Kotler could do was bring his arms up to try to

protect his face, his neck, his chest. It wouldn't matter. That... *thing*... in the man's hand would tear into Kotler's flesh.

There would be blood. And pain. And possibly death.

He waited for the blow.

Instead, he felt a rush of wind, and opened his eyes to see that the man was now pinned to the floor, with a woman on top of him.

Alex Kayne.

The man made a noise then—a guttural sort of growl—and with a strength belied by his frame he managed to raise his arms and throw Kayne aside.

She landed in a heap beside Kotler.

The man rose again, raised the blade, and was about to make an end to one or the other of them.

"Freeze!"

The voice came with a blast of light from Agent Barr's flashlight, and the man turned on him.

With no hesitation or fear, with a speed that was frightening, the man spun on his heel, whipping the blade outward.

Barr cried out, and a shot was fired, ricocheting wildly in a whine down the darkened corridor, disappearing into the guts of the mountain.

The man with the weapon turned and ran, also disappearing into that darkness.

Kotler scrambled to his feet and found the flashlight. He turned it in the direction the man had ran, and saw that there were dozens of side passages that way—side tunnels that would let someone escape in the maze of this place, untraceable. Especially if that someone happened to know these tunnels like the back of his hand.

He could be anywhere by now.

Kotler patted his coat, then reached inside. Holstered there was a 9mm Glock, issued to him by Historic Crimes with the very strict instructions that, as a civilian agent, he was never to pull it unless his life was in immediate danger.

He decided this counted.

"Roland!" Kotler shouted, over his shoulder. He was aiming the weapon, braced over his left wrist, while his left hand held the flashlight, aimed down the corridor. Still, no sign of movement.

"I'm here, Kotler," Denzel's voice came back.

Too quiet. Too calm.

Kotler spun around, holding the flashlight out, angling it so that he wouldn't blind anyone in the darkness.

He saw Denzel and Kayne kneeling on the floor.

Between them, as still as the air around them, was Agent Barr.

Kotler moved forward, glancing back over his shoulder to make sure the man with the blade wasn't nearby, taking advantage of their distraction.

When Kotler reached them, he let the 9mm and the flashlight drop to his side. There was enough light here to see what had happened.

Agent Barr lay in a pool of his own blood, which was still pouring from a gash in his throat. His eyes wide, one hand laying loosely near the wound, on his collar bone.

Still.

Unbreathing.

Dead.

Kotler turned again, raised the light and the 9mm, aiming down the corridor. "What do we do?" he asked, his tone cold. He had thoughts about the answer to this question.

Denzel took off his coat and lay it over Barr's face, then stood. He unholstered his own weapon, gripping it so tight that Kotler was sure it would crumble to dust in his hands.

"We hunt him," Denzel said.

Kotler nodded, then looked to Kayne.

She was pale. There was blood on her arms, her face.

"Al..." he'd been close to saying *Alex.*

"*Alicia,*" he corrected.

She didn't look up at him.

He glanced back to Denzel, then knelt beside Kayne.

"Alex," he whispered to her. "Are you hurt?"

She shook her head, looking up at him. Her eyes were brimmed with tears. "No. It's... his blood. I... I couldn't save him."

Kotler took in the scene now. She must have spotted that Barr was injured, had tried to staunch the bleeding with her hands. No use, Kotler knew. The wound had nicked the carotid artery. Barr had been dead in the time it had taken Kotler to get to his feet and draw his weapon. There would have been no way to save him.

He put a hand on Kayne's shoulder. "I'm sorry."

She shook her head, then wiped her eyes against the upper sleeve of her coat. It smeared blood across her face. "Don't be sorry," she said, clenching her jaw and standing. "Be mad."

Kotler nodded, joining her.

She had no weapon. Kotler might have thought she was innocent of the crimes for which she was accused, but even he hadn't been willing to arm a fugitive.

As he watched her, however, he realized she didn't need a weapon. She'd taken on the man with the blade—Andrew Jessup, the Comrade—with nothing but her bare hands, and had come out in better shape than anyone else.

She could take care of herself, Kotler realized. She didn't need a weapon—she *was* a weapon.

"Ok," he said, turning and joining Denzel, the 9mm and flashlight raised. "Let's go take down the Comrade."

CHAPTER EIGHT

Clara had fought and struggled and cried with frustration for more than three hours, but she was finally making progress.

The scraping had stopped, thank God.

But she hadn't.

She had found a can with a pull top and had pulled the ring to reveal it was baked beans. She hated baked beans.

But the prize wasn't the meal—it was the can top.

Bending it, using another can to pound it flat to get it into the right shape, she had painstakingly made a screwdriver.

She'd cut herself—twice—which had led to profuse bleeding, making her work both slippery and painful. But she'd pushed through that pain, and now she had it. A tool—one that would get her out of here.

She hoped. She prayed.

In the bouncing green light of the computer monitor, she surveyed her work. The world's ugliest screwdriver, to be sure. But it would do. It would *have* to do.

She had put it in her pocket and scaled the shelves, then crawled her way to the grate. And for hours now she had worked at the screws, pressing with all her strength, pushing her makeshift screwdriver into the grooves of the first screw and turning.

It didn't want to budge. It was locked in tight.

At first.

It took much longer than she'd wanted but slowly, slowly, centimeter by centimeter, it finally started to budge, to turn. Millimeters at a time, but it was *moving*.

It was painful. The can lid was cutting into her hands, and she'd finally torn a piece of cloth from her blouse to use as a handle. That helped, but only barely.

But the damned screw was *turning*.

After more than an hour, the first screw fell free, clacking and clattering on the metal shelf, rolling away into the darkness. She heard it bounce from shelf to shelf as it fell, then the sound of it hitting the concrete floor.

She laughed, but stifled it.

Too insane. It sounded too insane.

She took a shaky breath, felt her heart thumping hard enough she worried it would throw her off of the top shelf, and then got to work on the second screw.

This one seemed more stubborn than the first. She pressed and turned, putting all the pressure she could into it, putting her entire body weight into it. Everything she had was focused on that tiny, slender piece of metal.

And all... it had... to do... was... *turn dammit!*

Nothing. No movement.

She wept, moaning but stifling the sound. She fought the urge the fling the makeshift screwdriver into the darkness below.

This was getting to her. It was *too much.*

I'm going to die here!

Again the moan rose in her throat, this time completely out

of her control. There was no stifling it now, and she let her head drop to her knees, crouched there on the top shelf, scooting to lean back against the cinder block wall. Her only hope of escape stubbornly refused to budge, and she wasn't sure there was anything left in her to make it happen.

She sobbed.

This went on for some time—she wasn't sure how long. She had stopped paying attention to the clock which only reminded her of how dark this place was, how trapped she was.

But when the panic subsided, she sniffed, wiped at her nose with her sleeve, and started her work again.

More time. Hours? Maybe. Still nothing.

Out of frustration she screamed, raging at the screw, jamming the makeshift screwdriver into it and putting everything she had in trying to turn it—to no effect.

In utter frustration she reached out and grabbed the edges of the grate, working her fingers into the slender, tight gap she'd created by removing the first screw.

It hurt. The cuts on her fingers reopened, and blood oozed outward. The pressure of the metal grate biting into her skin was excruciating. She felt the edge of the cinderblock wall scrape her cuticles and knuckles. The pain fueled her anger, she screamed louder.

Suddenly, she realized, she had her fingers far enough into the gap that she could get a grip on it.

She pulled. She braced her feet against the cinderblock wall and pulled with her entire body.

The aluminum of the grate bent easily, swinging outward until she had it bent completely back against the wall. The stubborn screw still held, but she didn't care. She laughed, not even bothering to keep it in check, even as it sounded insane in her own ears.

She had her opening.

She tested it, reached inside, felt around. There was a sharp bend going upward, about four feet back. She could make that. If she crawled in on her back, she could sit up in that space. It would be a little claustrophobic, but she'd fit.

She did this, sliding in arms first, and then using her hands to help move herself forward the final few inches. She reached into the gap above, braced her hands against either side of the shaft, and then wriggled her way into a sitting position, getting her feet into the grate. From there she worked her way up to a standing position, scraping her knees on the bend of the shaft but otherwise getting upright easily.

There was nothing but pitch blackness here. She couldn't even see the light from the screensaver anymore—that damnable light that had marked her captivity with an eerie, uncaring glow—and suddenly she *missed* it.

She felt the fear rising, felt the scream, just about to start. She was *freaking out*—panicking, about to have a full on anxiety attack.

She stopped. She took several deep breaths. She calmed herself, resolved herself.

She'd have to feel her way from here, that was all. That was easy. That was ok.

It was that, or go back down.

Go back to that room, to that bouncing green clock, to that scraping sound.

Back to being trapped.

Back to being a prisoner.

No, she decided.

It was firm. It was bold. She was afraid, so very afraid. But she would *do this*.

She took another deep breath, felt around in the shaft above her, and then pressed her feet and hands against metal, lifting herself upward.

She might end up trapped in this vent.

That thought sent a fresh panic through her guts. She *might* end up dying in this narrow, confined space, buried under five miles of New Mexico stone, never to be seen or heard from again. A rotting, moldering corpse no one would ever notice. A smell in the air conditioning that would fade with time.

She might.

But she might not.

She might, instead, find some way out.

And that was all the encouragement, all the *hope,* that she needed.

She climbed higher and higher, pressing against either side of the shaft, using friction to keep moving upward until she found another shaft running back in the same direction as the room below.

Was this it? Was this a way out?

She felt her heart thump, and squeezed herself into the shaft, moving forward, the anticipation—the hope—building.

If this wasn't the way out, it was least a way to leave that room behind. That scraping behind.

She crawled in complete darkness, with nothing but her hands and her hope guiding her.

She wasn't sure where this would take her, or what she would find when she got there. But it was her own choice, her own direction. Whatever happened next, at least she had some control.

She crawled on.

CHAPTER NINE

Symon and Mayher had been told to wait.

Ricky Greer—Andrew Jessup's former landlord—was in with his doctor. They'd be alerted when he was free to receive visitors.

They waited, though Symon didn't feel altogether comfortable.

This place reminded him of the senior care facility where his grandparents had died. He remembered visiting them, as a kid. The smell of places like this—a cloying mixture of disinfectant and cafeteria food—always bothered him. He knew it wasn't quite rational, but the smell reminded him of something sick in the air.

Death in the air.

And the people, the elderly in these places, were always a little too eager to talk to a young kid. They would corner him, smiling and talking to him in strange, sing-song tones, as if he were two, not twelve. It was like they saw in him something they'd lost, something they were trying to reclaim. Like they wanted to suck the youth from him, and return to a better time in their lives.

Symon wasn't a fan of these places. And when his grandparents had died, he'd sworn them off. His father had passed several years ago, leaving only his mother. She was approaching the age when she'd need care, and Symon had already arranged for live-in help. It would cost him half his paycheck each month, but he'd sooner live out of his car than see his mother in a place like this.

"Agents?" a nurse called to them, then gestured for them to follow.

Symon and Mayher were led down a corridor lined with doors and various pieces of medical equipment. Nurses moved at officious paces, orderlies pushed carts carrying everything from food to cleaning supplies. The occasional doctor stepped out into the hall, checking charts, jotting notes, and moving on to the next.

Eventually Symon and Mayher were ushered into Ricky Greer's room.

The man looked like he was about to pass at any second. He looked like death on pause.

Thin to the point of his bones showing through his skin, his head all but bald, wispy threads of grey hair combed loosely over to the side—Greer wore an oxygen mask and had an IV drip embedded in his arm. He was pale to the point of being blue. And though his eyes did still have some brightness, Symon thought it might be due more to whatever chemical cocktail was flowing into the man's veins. He was lucid by prescription. Possibly the only thing keeping him from drifting away in his sleep.

They had been briefed on Greer's condition beforehand, but it was still tough to see. Too familiar. Too much like nightmares Symon still had, his grandfather trussed up in tubes and wires, a thin hospital gown providing nothing more than pitiful modesty, and even that veil pierced as nurses roughly moved him, shift his position, removed all dignity from his final hours.

Symon took a quick, deep breath, quickly clearing his throat, steeling himself. This was not the time for his personal garbage. They had a job to do here.

"Mr. Greer," Symon said, "thank you for agreeing to see us."

Greer was sitting up, and he nodded without quite looking at them. His eyes looked deep and dark, but there was some spark there. He finally glanced their way, having huffed oxygen for a moment, as if preparing himself for what came next. He reached an age-spotted hand upward, pulling down the oxygen mask.

"You're here..." he gasped a breath, coughed, shook his head. "You're here about... the Comrade."

"Andrew Jesup," Mayher nodded.

"Did you... find him?" Greer asked.

Mayher shook her head. "Not yet. We're hoping you can help with that."

Greer shook his head as well. "Haven't seen him in... more than twenty years. Guy still... owes me money." He laughed at this last bit, which turned into a coughing fit. He pushed the oxygen mask back over his face and inhaled in ragged, rattling breaths until the coughing and wheezing subsided.

"Don't ever... smoke," Greer warned, shaking his head as he pulled the mask back down.

"Mr. Greer," Symon said, "you told the police that you found Jesup's apartment ransacked. Do you recall whether anyone had reason to attack or abduct him?"

Greer laughed again, which in turn made him cough. He shook his head as the phlegmy sound of the laughter faded.

"Everyone," he said. "Everyone had... a reason. I had a reason. Anyone who ever... met the commie bastard."

"Was it all about his Communism?" Mayher asked. "People hated him for that?"

"That was part of it," Greer said, taking a moment to suck air from the mask. "But the guy was... just a creep. Scared people. I was ready to kick him out, when he... disappeared. I figured he probably just skipped out without paying the rent. But I found out... that if I filed a police report, I could collect insurance. So, that's what I did."

"So you don't suspect any sort of foul play," Symon said.

Greer waved a hand, dismissive. "Nah. If anyone was doing something... wrong, it was the Comrade himself. Guy was a... thief."

"You had proof of that?" Mayher asked.

"Stole stuff all the time," Greer said. He took another hit of oxygen. "My other tenants... used to complain about it. Stupid stuff, though. They'd come home and find that somebody broke in... and took all their *toilet paper*. Stuff like that. But he was stealing gas out of their cars, too. Caught him... on that one."

Mayher exchanged a glance with Symon.

Symon nodded. This gelled with what Alfred Cox had told them.

The conversation went on like this for several more minutes until a nurse eventually came in to tell them their time was up. Doctor's orders.

They nodded and made ready to leave.

"Wait... a minute," Greer gasped. "Just another thing. Just... remembered it. About a... year ago, I saw him. Swore it was him."

"Saw him?" Symon asked. "Where?"

"In town. Leaving the library. Had a bunch of books and

dumped them into that old pickup of his. 'S'how I... knew it was him." Greer coughed and took another hit of oxygen.

"I was just turning around, was going to stop him... talk to him. Ask him for the money he owed me. Had... hospital bills to pay." He motioned at the room around him. "But he got into the pickup and drove off. Bat outta hell. I followed him for a bit, until he turned off the main road, heading toward the mountains. Last time I ever saw him."

"Do you know where he turned?" Mayher asked.

Greer thought for a moment, then gave directions and road numbers. "It wasn't no official road," he said. "Just a dirt track. Used to be... military. Old base, I think. Fences are gone, but the road... still there."

Mayher was taking notes, and Symon was about to ask a follow-up question when the nurse insisted it was time to leave.

They did so, and when they were back in their car they started talking over what they'd learned.

"I don't think there's any doubt that Andrew Jesup is the man with the face tattoo, from Dr. Rivers' text message," Mayher said.

"Agreed," Symon said.

"So, what next?" Mayher asked. "This isn't exactly a case breaking lead. We pretty much already knew everything Greer had to tell us."

Symon was thinking. Mayher was right. Confirming Jesup's identity wasn't much of an accomplishment. Their conversation with Greer didn't give them anything new to work from. It really just left Symon and Mayher at a dead end of sorts. Nothing much to follow up on.

"Greer said Jesup left the main road and drove into the mountains," Symon said.

Mayher nodded.

"We're thinking that Jesup is confirmed as the face tattoo,"

Symon replied. "So we can assume that he was headed for the Pit."

Mayher was studying him, then nodded slowly. "If you say so."

"I don't see anything to do but follow up on this lead," Symon said.

Mayher blinked. "What lead? You... you mean go to the Pit?"

"Into the mountains. Jesup's last known location."

"Yeah, a *year* ago," Mayher said.

Symon shrugged. "We go where the evidence takes us. Right now, this is all we got. We've followed cold trails before."

"I can't think of any that were much colder," Mayher said.

Symon looked at her. "You don't have to go."

She thought about this. "Are you nuts? Of course I have to go. Someone has to back you up."

Symon smiled, then turned their car around.

"Where are we going?" Mayher asked.

"To get something more appropriate for going off-road," Symon replied.

CHAPTER TEN

Agent Denzel hadn't been kidding.

Kayne followed along behind the agent and Dr. Kotler, both men moving in unison, weapons raised, flashlights casting beams out ahead of them. Denzel was on the left and Kotler was on the right, and each took whatever corridor came up on their side, turning into it, covered by the other.

They didn't go far. Just a few feet. Far enough to get an idea, to see if they could spot the Comrade.

She had to admit, it was impressive to see them in action. They obviously knew and trusted each other at a deep level—knew what the other was thinking, what the other needed. For an archaeologist, Kayne thought Kotler was pretty good at this kind of thing. But then, that made sense.

She'd seen everything there was on file about Dan Kotler. His past. The training he'd gone through. The secret order in which his grandfather had been a high-ranking member.

There was a lot more to Dan Kotler than mere archaeology.

Kayne lingered back as the two men scanned and explored

ahead of them. She watched closely, paying attention, picked out details, trying to keep her mind off of all the blood.

She hadn't been able to save him.

Agent Barr had bled out under her hands, as she'd frantically pressed his neck, trying to staunch the bleeding any way she could.

She could tell right away that it wasn't enough.

There had been blood on her hands before. The blood of men who had tried to hurt her, tried to use her. She knew when death was inevitable.

She wouldn't let herself think about it.

She followed along, letting the two men ahead of her scan and clear their path. They would run out of corridor soon. The Comrade had to have taken one of these side passages, to escape deeper into the mountain. He knew this compound far better than they did. He would know where to hide, how to keep out of their reach. This was going to be a long, dangerous search.

Kotler and Denzel were ahead of her when she heard something.

It came from one of the side corridors—an odd sound, nothing like she was expecting. It was the sort of noise metal made when flexing.

She turned her flashlight on, shined it down the corridor, and noted that a series of exposed air vents and conduits were suspended from the ceiling in that direction.

"Guys," she said, too quietly. "*Guys!*"

Kotler and Denzel stopped and turned, their flashlights nearly blinding her.

"Something down this corridor," she said, shading her eyes with one hand while pointing her own flashlight in the direction of the sound.

They moved toward her. "You're sure?" Kotler asked. "We just cleared that one."

"I... heard something. It came from the vents, I think."

They all entered the corridor, watchful, keeping their eyes roving. They stopped at the nearest conduit, each raising their lights toward the ceiling.

The sound came again—a flexing, echoing sound, in the distance.

"I'd recognize that anywhere," Kotler said. "Someone is in that vent."

"The Comrade?" Denzel asked.

Kotler shook his head. "I don't think so. Look at it," he shined his light along the conduit, and stepped under it to illuminate it from the other side. "Someone small. Lean. It's probably Dr. Rivers."

Kayne felt her heart pound. Rivers was in the vents?

Kayne has spent plenty of time crawling around in air vents herself, evading capture, infiltrating the offices of a target. It wasn't quite the experience that movies and television made it out to be. In most cases, air vents and duct work were far too small for anyone to move around in. Someone slight and trim might be able to do it in industrial systems, such as the one in this base. But there were dangers and problems to deal with, even if you fit.

She glanced around her at the pressing darkness. The entire building was locked down, lights off. It was as dark as a well inside those conduits. Rivers had to be feeling her way around, blind. And every move meant facing unseen danger.

She had to be scared out of her mind.

But more than that...

"At least she's safe," Kayne said, relief in her voice.

"Safe?" Denzel asked.

"She's right," Kotler said. "If Rivers is crawling around in the ducts, it means she's alive, and the Comrade can't get to her. For now."

"So what do we do?" Denzel asked. "Can we contact her? Is she close?"

Kayne shook her head. "I don't think so. The sound—I think it's just echoing to this point. She may be in the area, but she's not *here*. And if we try to contact her, it may just call her location out to the Comrade."

Denzel thought about this, then nodded. "Alright. We still need to find her, make contact with her. But the danger is that the Comrade is around somewhere, armed and dangerous."

"We should split up," Kotler said.

"Not on your life," Denzel replied. "We've already lost Barr..."

"Roland, it's the only way," Kotler insisted. "We have to keep searching for the Comrade and take him out. But we need to make contact with Rivers, to make sure she's safe and to get her out of here. I don't see how we do both, if we stay together."

Denzel was again shaking his head.

"I'll go for Rivers," Kayne said.

"You're unarmed," Denzel said. "And also, no."

"We'll both go," Kotler said, holding up his weapon demonstrably. "Roland..."

Denzel had a sour expression on his face. "Kotler, I swear to God, you plan this stuff."

Kotler chuckled. "Please," he said, "I'm not much of a planner. And I'm not in any rush to meet Mr. Choppy Blade Thingy in the dark again."

"That makes two of us," Kayne said.

"But you know this is our best shot," Kotler continued.

"We have no comms," Denzel replied.

Kayne took a breath and stepped forward. "Actually, that's not entirely true."

She held up her phone.

"No signal in here," Denzel replied.

"There is," Kayne said. "It just isn't what you're expecting. I found it when we first got here. Sort of an ancestor to LTE. I have a program on my phone that can open it up for us to use for communication. It'll allow us to stay in contact."

Denzel looked from her to Kotler, then back again. "I knew it," he said.

Kayne felt something chill within her.

"Knew... what?" Kotler asked.

Denzel nodded to Kayne. "Her. She's not Alicia Carter, is she? That's Alex Kayne."

Kotler and Kayne exchanged glances, then looked back to Denzel.

"Roland..." Kotler started.

"Save it. I suspected it before we even left," Denzel said, scowling. "But I wasn't positive." He squared off with Kayne. "I've read your file. And I've talked to Dr. Ludlum about you. I know who you are, and I know that you're operating as a CI for Historic Crimes. But you know... when this is over... I don't have a choice."

Kayne studied him, then pursed her lips, nodding. "I know."

Denzel glared at Kotler. "And you knew," he said.

Kotler shrugged. "I still have no idea what you're talking about."

"Kotler..."

"But," Kotler interrupted. "If this *is* Alex Kayne, so far she's been an asset. She saved me from the Comrade. She tried to save Agent Barr's life. And she's the one who heard Rivers moving around in the duct work. I'm not sure a fugitive would do any of those things, personally. So really, Roland, unless you've made a positive ID..."

He stopped, waiting.

Kayne felt her heart pounding.

Denzel looked from each of them, then made a disgusted sound. "Loopholes," the agent growled. "You're always falling back on loopholes."

He turned to Kayne, looming over her, his jaw tight. "Of course... I have to be mistaken. I have no way of making a positive ID at this time. So of course, I apologize... Dr. Carter."

He glared at Kotler.

"Of course," Kayne said, affecting more courage than she actually felt. "So now that we've settled that, one sec..."

She used her phone, giving QuIEK the command to open the ancient LTE signal on both Denzel's and Kotler's phones. She also had it link to Kotler's iPad, in the 4x4 outside. Just in case. That signal might act as a relay for them to call out and maybe bring help. It was a bit of a long shot, since the Pit's signal wasn't connecting to local cell towers. But she'd cross that bridge when the time came.

"Ok, we'll be able to chat," Kayne said. "You can use the phone like a walkie talkie. Just raise to talk."

"Neat trick," Denzel said. "They're teaching interesting things to the computer forensics team these days."

"We like to stay nimble, sir," Kayne replied.

Denzel again looked between the two of them and grumbled. "Great. I thought having one of you around was a nuisance."

"Stay safe, Roland," Kotler said. "Just... remember to breathe."

Kayne had noted from Denzel's file that the agent suffered from claustrophobia. It had slipped her mind—he hadn't shown any signs of it, that she could tell. But on top of being a world-class expert in reading body language, Dr. Kotler knew Agent

Denzel better than anyone. If the agent showed even the slightest sign of stress, Kotler would know.

Denzel waved him off as he turned and moved back to the main corridor, weapon and flashlight raised. "I'm fine. You just make sure you take care of Dr. Carter. I'll have some questions for her, later." He left them standing under the conduit as he moved deeper into the Pit.

Kotler looked at Kayne. "Just you and me now," he said. "Ready for this?"

"Ready to risk being slashed to death by a psychotic communist, in a secret, defunct military base, five miles under a mountain, so I can be arrested when it's all over?" She shrugged. "Sure. It's basically a Saturday for me."

Kotler smiled, chuckled lightly, and the two of them moved toward the distant sound of what they hoped was a safe and protected Dr. Clara Rivers.

CHAPTER ELEVEN

THE ROAD to the Pit was paved with bad indentions.

Potholes the size of moon craters made the terrain all but impassable. Even in the 4x4, the going was slow and jarring. Less than half an hour in, Symon worried their bones might liquify, and a rescue team would fly in to find two puddles in the floorboard.

Which was why he was relieved when Mayher discovered that there was a hidden side-road, just over the hill.

They had stopped to get their bearings, to make sure nothing had rattled off of the 4x4, or off of themselves, when Mayher had slipped away, climbing one of the short hills and disappearing behind the brush. Symon didn't bother questioning why.

But when she reappeared, she excitedly called for him to join her on the hilltop.

He did so, clambering up the loose gravel, up over the bigger stones, until he stood by her side at the top of the hill. She pointed.

"That's not on the map," Symon frowned.

Stretching before them was what appeared to be a level and grated road, running from horizon to horizon, hidden by the hills themselves.

"Seems to be going in the same general direction," Mayher said.

Symon agreed. He turned and estimated the path it would take to get from the known road to this new, seemingly better one.

"This makes sense," he said, after a moment.

"What makes sense?" Mayher asked.

"From what we've uncovered, Jesup has to be making regular trips in and out of here. And Dr. Rivers had to have had a path in that wasn't so rough—she was in a rental sedan, not a 4x4. There would have to be something other than this Braille strip of a road, or she would never have made it to the Pit in one piece."

"So Jesup made his own road?" Mayher asked.

"Or improvised one. And he kept it a secret. I doubt anyone has used the actual road for decades until Agent Denzel's team went this way."

Mayher nodded. "Ok, then. So, I vote we make our way to this smoother road and go from here."

Symon agreed, and the two of them scrambled back to the 4x4, then drove it through a narrow pass that allowed them to gain access to the other side of the hills.

The going was much faster now, and much less bone jarring. There was still the occasional bump or trench, but it was navigable. Most of the terrain was solid rock, from what Symon could determine, and though there were points where they were driving at a distinct and almost impossible angle, they never encountered impassible terrain.

In no time, they arrived at the coordinates of the Pit where they found the 4x4 that Agent Denzel's team had used to get there. They searched and found Dr. Rivers's rental car as well.

But no sign of anyone, or of where they'd gone. Worse, there was no sign of a base. Not so much as an outbuilding was visible.

"Ok..." Mayher said, confused.

"The facility has to be here somewhere," Symon said. "Kayne's data says there are multiple entrances."

"So how do we find them?" Mayher asked.

Symon shrugged. "We look."

The next hour was spent combing the hillside, looking for any sign of an opening. There were potential hits, including a small cave that dead-ended less than twenty feet in. But there was nothing that seemed to suggest "defunct secret government facility."

They regrouped back at the vehicles.

"Something tells me the entrance is right under our nose," Symon huffed, taking a long pull from a bottle of water.

Mayher was standing with her back to him, slowly scanning the hillside. She turned, shaking her head. "Maybe we're going about this all wrong," she said.

"How so?"

"Agent Denzel and the others got into this place. We can assume that, right?"

Symon nodded.

"So they must have had... I don't know... a key or something. Dr. Rivers said something in her text message about the Decalogue stone and quantum encryption. So maybe there was some kind of technology involved?"

Symon considered this. "Denzel brought a computer forensics expert with him. Maybe she found a way to crack the security of this place?"

"Too bad we didn't bring an expert of our own," Mayher

said.

Symon huffed and shook his head. "Maybe we did."

He took out his phone and held it up, inspecting the signal he was getting.

One bar.

Thin. Anemic. Barely there.

He tried getting online, but was having trouble. Everything was slow to the point of being useless. He tried sending a text to Kayne, at one of the numbers she'd given him. Seconds later he got an alert that the message had failed to send.

"Ok then," he said. "I guess that's not going to work."

He was about to slip the phone back into his pocket when, on a whim, he opened the settings to scan for Wi-Fi. It was habit, when his LTE signal was low. More of an impulse than a serious plan. But when the Wi-Fi settings opened, he got a hit.

Kotler iPad, the display read.

"You've got to be kidding me," he said, showing the phone to Mayher.

"Must be close, then," Mayher said.

Symon nodded, and the two of them resumed their search, this time on the lookout for Dr. Kotler's smart tablet.

They reached the 4x4 that Denzel and team had driven into the area, and when Symon tried the rear door it opened without hesitation.

"Just left it unlocked?" Mayher asked.

"Bad protocol, but maybe it'll be a lucky break for us."

He leaned into the 4x4 and started sifting through the back seat. He came across a leather case that contained several documents and, thankfully, Kotler's iPad.

Lifting it up, Symon touched the screen.

"Locked," he said. "But..."

"What is it?" Mayher asked.

"Full signal," he said, shaking his head. "It's connected to a tower or something."

He held it up for Mayher to see and was about to comment when a voice—a familiar voice—came out of the iPad's speakers.

"Eric?"

Symon blinked, exchanging glances with Mayher.

"Eric, is that you?"

Alex Kayne's voice. He'd recognize it anywhere.

"Alex? Where... how?"

"We're inside!" Kayne said. "Eric, thank God you're here. There's a lunatic in here. Armed. Very dangerous. Did you bring backup?"

"*In here?*" Symon asked. "Alex... are you saying you're here, in New Mexico? You're *in the Pit?*"

"Long story short," a male voice came over the speaker, "She's with me."

"Dr. Kotler?" Symon asked.

"Hello, Agent Symon," Kotler said. "It's good to hear your voice."

"What the hell is going on?" Mayher asked.

Kayne spoke from the iPad. "We're inside the Pit, and Agent Barr was murdered by the Comrade. Right now, it's looking like that won't be his last victim."

"How do we help?" Symon asked, suddenly more alert to his surroundings. "We can't find the way in."

"One second..." Kayne replied.

After only a moment there was a slight rumble in the ground, and suddenly a part of the hillside rose and moved away. Symon and Mayher stood back, watching, then looking at each other, confused.

"Welcome to the Pit, Agent Symon," Kotler's voice said. "Keep your eyes open for a psychopath with a very sharp blade."

CHAPTER TWELVE

Clara had been crawling blind for hours when she heard the gunshots.

She froze, waiting, listening. From where she was, there was no way to know where the sounds had come from. They were muffled and distant, deflected by miles of metal ducts. They could be coming from anywhere. But she recognized them instantly.

What did they mean?

She hadn't seen any guns since coming to the Pit. And the man—the Comrade—had that long, ugly blade. As far as she knew, it was just the two of them down here. So who was firing? And what—or who—were they shooting at?

Her heart pounded. Her brain buzzed with one word.

Rescue!

She had been moving quietly, painfully, through the duct work, trying to keep the sound of her passage to a minimum. It was excruciating and exhausting. But she'd plodded on, feeling her way along, praying with all she had that she would eventually find some way out.

Now, with the sound of gunfire providing some sort of hope, she increased her speed, and with it the noise of her passage.

It was like crawling through a baking tin. Every movement flexed the metal, which echoed loudly around her. She couldn't hear the gunfire anymore, but wasn't sure if it was because it had stopped or because she was drowning it out.

She kept moving.

Eventually she came to a split in the ductwork—something she'd encountered a number of times since crawling in here. She felt the possible paths with her hands, reaching into the dark in both directions, trying to find some clue about where to go next.

She would have to choose, left or right.

She took a few deep breaths and turned left.

For the next several minutes she crawled as she had from the start, until finally she came to a vent.

Dead end.

She felt her heart pounding, and put her hands against the vent, pushing.

She knew from experience that there were two screws holding the vent in place, from the outside. Just one of them had been a legitimate pain to remove, when she'd climbed in from the storage room. Here, from inside the duct, there would be no way to remove the screws.

She was going to have to force her way out.

Her only hope was that the screws give with enough pressure from this side.

She was pushing, feeling that pressure against her palms, and feeling twice that amount growing in her chest, when there was a sudden, sickening, rending sound from somewhere beyond her feet, in the darkness of the shaft.

She felt the shaft itself tremble and shake, and she strained her eyes and her neck, twisting her body to see if she could spot anything in that endless darkness.

Smack-squeeeee!

The sound was hideous, like a thousand metal fingernails on a chalkboard. The racket forced her jaw to clench.

It was the sound of metal tearing.

She redoubled her efforts, pushing frantically against the grate in front of her, slamming her palms into it over and over until they ached.

Squeeeeeee!

More tearing, and she once again spared a glance down the length of her body.

This time she could see.

A light, pouring in from a gash in the conduit a few feet from her toes. Someone had ripped the metal open, and light was pouring in from the outside.

She watched as a face appeared, swathed in shadow, but she could still make out that hideous tattoo in a passing glint of light.

The Comrade.

She screamed, and resumed pounding on the grate in front of her, even as she kicked and thrashed her legs at the face of the man below.

The grate was starting to give, but not enough. Not fast enough.

She looked back to see the Comrade reaching into the maw of metal he had created, his hands stretching to reach for her legs. She was too far, just too far, for him to reach her, thank God.

She saw the hook of the man's blade rise into the shaft, light reflecting dully from its crimson crescent.

She again pounded on the grate, pushing, hitting, ignoring the pain.

She felt something sharp knick at her left calf and screamed again. It hadn't gotten her. It had merely torn through her pant leg and scraped her skin. But the Comrade would try again. He would hook her flesh and drag her screaming through a womb of jagged metal, to be born into the hell below.

She screamed in fury now, and rose on her elbows, drawing herself forward and slamming the grate with her head, like a battering ram.

It hurt, and she saw stars, but as the blackness oozed and swirled around her, she heard a clatter of metal on a concrete floor.

The grate had broken free, and she was laying with her eyes and nose overhanging the outer ledge.

She scrambled again, hearing the Comrade shout, hearing the sound of the blade coming down hard on bare metal, scraping in a long screech that echoed through the ductwork and into the room where Clara now found herself.

She had poured out of the duct and had barely gotten her hands out in front of her before hitting the floor. She rolled, landing on her back, the fallen grating under her, painful and biting.

She was banged up, scraped up, and bruised to every square inch.

She was still trapped in this place, miles below the surface.

But she was alive.

And she had gotten away from the Comrade and his blade.

She laughed.

She cried.

She got to her feet, limping and exploring, this new place, looking for anything that might help her, that she might be able to use to defend herself.

The sound from the ductwork had ceased, which meant the Comrade was coming here. Wherever here was.

She felt around until her hands met something astonishing. Something she could barely believe.

A light switch.

She huffed a few breaths laced with prayers and then flipped the switch to on.

She blinked in the explosion of light. Tears came to her eyes, from the brightness but more from the relief. She had not seen light in days. She had seen only darkness, and more chasing her.

These lights—fluorescent tubes that buzzed with a green-tinged hue—were as beautiful as the heavens.

She was in an office.

No windows. But there was a large piece of artwork on one wall—a depiction of the Los Lunas mountains themselves, cast in light from a golden sunset, looking far more idyllic than the outside ever really managed, in Clara's opinion.

There was a desk and office chair, and the wall to the right of this was lined floor to ceiling with cabinets and shelves. A round table with two chairs occupied the other corner of the room.

And then there was the door.

She raced to it, cracked it open, peered outside. The light from overhead cast a wedge of visibility into the hall. There was nothing to see there.

It took everything she had not to rush out there, to try to flee. She needed something first. Needed many things, but one thing in particular.

A weapon.

She pushed the door closed and engaged the lock in its handle. Not much. Flimsy. She pulled the desk across the floor and against the door, just in case.

She searched.

There wasn't much left behind when the government

cleared this place, from what she could tell. Mostly just the detritus of bureaucracy—reams of notepads, mountains of paperclips and other office supplies. Given that this facility was from the 1990s, she might be looking at a billion dollars worth of paperclips, in terms of government spending. But it was all worthless trash, at the moment.

No weapons.

What she did find, in the cabinet along one wall, was an old fashioned paper cutter—the sort with a large, bladed swing arm.

She worked at it, applied pressure, wriggled it back and forth until the blade snapped from its hinge. She huffed from the effort, but gripped her prize in her hand.

The Comrade had his blade.

And now Clara had hers.

She hefted it a few times. Felt the edge. Not seriously sharp, but enough to do some damage. It felt like something she could handle. The Comrade wouldn't be expecting it, anyway. It would do. It would have to do.

But there was one other piece of treasure she found in her rifling—something that gave her even more hope than a weapon in hand.

A flashlight.

Small—just a pen light, a tiny key chain that wasn't meant for much more than illuminating a darkened keyhole or peering into a desk drawer. This one had the logo of a hotel on it—obviously swag from some conference. But the batteries were still good, and it still provided a nice little cone of light. It would also do.

Armed and illuminated, Clara moved back to the desk in front of the door. She had done her work quickly, frantically, but there still may have been enough time for the Comrade to have found his way to her.

Before she moved that desk and opened that door, she needed a plan.

She looked around again at the pile of discarded office supplies. She spotted what she needed—the exact distraction she'd need—next to the now-broken paper cutter.

She grabbed it, and slid it into her belt, at the base of her back. At an angle, so she would move freely. But it was there. Close. Easy to reach.

She moved the desk now, slowly and cautiously, and then cracked open the door.

No sign of him. The Comrade hadn't yet made it to this corridor.

She let out a sigh of relief and then moved out into the hallway. She left the light on. It would help, and it might even draw the Comrade toward it, away from wherever she was.

The space she was moving into was a small suite of cubicles, looking every bit like a standard office space. There were even motivational posters hanging from some of the cubical walls, abandoned with everything else when this place closed shop, more than two decades earlier.

Clara gripped the paper cutter blade in her right hand and kept the small flashlight turned off and dangling by its strap from her left wrist. Enough light poured out from the office to illuminate the cubicle farm well enough, though the demountable walls made for a maze of danger all around her.

Scraaaaaaaape.

She felt her blood go cold. She knew that sound, all too well. The last time she'd heard it, she'd been trapped in that storage room, her only source of light the bouncing clock on the computer's display. It was a sound that triggered deep, anxious fear. It was a sound that made her want to scream, to hide, to curl up some place safe and pray and wait and moan.

It was a sound that pissed her off. A sound that made her want—*need*—to fight back.

She gripped the paper cutter blade, her hand clenching it so tight she thought it might liquify.

She slipped her left hand back, taking hold of her distraction there, sliding it from her belt, holding it tight but letting her fingers find the plastic lip, the edge that would open it.

Thus doubly armed, she waited.

Scraaaaaaape.

She turned in the direction of the sound—that noise that was meant to terrify her and make her run, scurrying the other way.

She moved toward it.

The Comrade, apparently sensing things were not going the way he intended, stepped out from one of the darkened cubicles. He was still deep enough in the darkness that Clara couldn't make out the details of his face, but there was one part of him that was caught by the light, that he ensured could be seen.

The disgusting, wicked curve of the blade.

He spoke then, and his voice was a low hiss, gravely to the point of being a challenge to understand. "This is Móki," he said, raising the blade slightly. "She thirsts."

Clara felt like throwing up. The fear within her tore at her guts, and she felt skin flush, sweat breaking out all over her body.

She was a trained agent. She'd gone through basic hand-to-hand combat. She felt she could take care of herself.

But that blade. That hook. That red-encrusted, jagged metal.

She held up her one blade. "This is Paper Cutter," she said, trying to sound far more brave than she felt. She swallowed. "He hates assholes."

There was no sound from the Comrade, but he suddenly rushed forward, the wicked blade rising up as the man's arms crossed his chest. He intended to rake it across her throat, she could tell. He would slash her throat and leave her gurgling and bleeding out and dying on the floor at his feet and *screw him!*

With more speed and force than she realized she'd been capable of, Clara raised her distraction, lifting it up and outward, and then slamming it with all her might across the Comrade's forehead.

He'd been about to slash at her when the thing struck.

Suddenly he staggered back as a cloud of confetti exploded around his head, as thousands of tiny, paper circles erupted from the three-hole punch.

Clara let the thing clatter to the floor, and took full advantage of the distraction as she sprinted past the Comrade, out of the cubicle farm and into the darkened corridors beyond.

She clicked on the little flashlight, and used it to navigate a series of quick turns, getting as much distance between her and the Comrade as possible.

He screamed in rage behind her, and she knew he was in pursuit. She knew she'd have to find another hiding place, to turn off the flashlight, to keep herself quiet and calm and hidden. Again.

She gripped the paper cutter, and ducked into a room that was absolutely crammed with books—unorganized stacks of them, spilling from shelves, rising from mounds in the floor. Paperbacks of every description, well-read and well worn.

She dropped behind one mountain of them, turned off the flashlight, and held a hand over her mouth, breathing slowly, trying to calm herself. Waiting.

Scraaaaaaaape.

The sound came from outside of the little library, somewhere out in the corridor.

Scraaaaaaape.

The same game. The same tactic.

It made her angry, which helped her fight back the fear.

The Comrade was still out there. Still had all the advantages. But he only knew a few tricks.

Clara was smart. All she would have to do was wait and think. That was her hope.

Someone else was here, too, she remembered. Someone had fired weapons. If they survived, they'd be looking for her.

She settled in behind the stack of paperbacks closest to her, gripped the paper cutter, and focused on trying to stay calm.

CHAPTER THIRTEEN

"Do you hear that?" Kayne asked.

Kotler tilted his head, listening.

They had been following the air duct as closely as possible, though at times it disappeared into walls that seemed six feet thick, and picking up the trail again was a matter of guessing, at best. For more than an hour now, they had done their best to try to keep it in sight, and they were failing.

Now they were hearing something that sent a chill down Kotler's spine.

Scraaaaape!

Hideous, metal-on-metal, coming from somewhere ahead of them, in the darkness.

Following that sound came a cacophony of noises that they couldn't identify.

Kotler gripped his weapon tighter as the two of them raced forward, rushing toward the noise.

"Maybe I should call Roland," Kotler said as they cautiously made their way into a series of halls and cubicles.

He picked the phone out of his pocket and raised it to his

lips.

"Roland," he said, waiting.

"Kotler?"

"We may have a situation," Kotler replied. "I think the Comrade is here."

"Where are you?" Denzel replied.

Kotler opened his mouth to reply, then stopped, looking at Kayne.

She shrugged. "I have no idea."

"That's going to be a tough question to answer, Roland. We followed the ductwork pretty deep into this facility, but we've had some side trails." He looked around, trying to find a landmark. "It looks like we're in a suite of office cubicles. Same level. I'm not seeing anything to identify where we are."

There was a pause from the other end which Kotler knew from history meant that Denzel was cursing Kotler's name. "Stay put. I'm on my way. *Do not engage.*"

"Sure thing," Kotler said.

"We're going to engage, though, right?" Kayne asked.

"Oh, I don't see how we could avoid it," Kotler replied, smiling.

They moved deeper into the cubicle farm, quietly, slowly.

"What about Agents Symon and Mayher?" Kotler asked. "They're making their way in…"

"I doubt they'd get here in time," Kayne said. "We're pretty deep. They'll find their way here, eventually."

Kotler nodded, then the two of them moved forward, toward the racket.

Ahead of them they could see light.

An office door stood open, light pouring from it out into the array of cubicles. It was such an odd and ordinary scene, like visiting an office building after hours. It made Kotler feel a bit disoriented.

There was more noise from up ahead.

Scraaaaaape.

Kotler trained his flashlight on the spot where he thought the noise might be originating, but that direction presented only more office space—cubicles, file cabinets, and a few doors that could lead to anywhere.

"It's curious..." Kotler said, quietly.

Kayne, standing beside him, gave him a look.

"The Comrade came here and took this place over. From all evidence, he's made it his perfect home. Repurposing spaces and materials into whatever he needed. He's been here for years, and he's taken over the entire complex. But this space... it's almost untouched."

Kayne looked around, sweeping the beam of her own flashlight over the cubicle walls.

Kotler noted that there were still posters and artwork on the walls of the place. Still personal items on some of the desks. But no sign of dust. The environment here was closed, the air apparently filtered and recycled. But even that wouldn't be enough to keep at least some dust from collecting on every surface here.

If anything, it looked like someone had been keeping it up, cleaning and maintaining the cubicles.

"The Comrade is keeping an office space?" Kayne asked.

"I... think it's some sort of..." he was working through it, shaking his head. "Well, as hard as it is to believe, I think it's a sort of shrine. To an enemy, I think."

"A shrine to an enemy?" Kayne asked. "Who would do that? I thought you only built shrines for gods or whatever."

Kotler shrugged. "Many cultures have shrines that serve a variety of purposes, from honoring a fallen loved one to worshiping gods, and even cursing enemies. In West African Vodun—one of the origins of Voodoo—practitioners would sometimes build shrines as part of a curse on an enemy. Judging from the look and layout of this place, the Comrade tends to it, keeps it in order. I think maybe he sees this as symbolic of his enemies—capitalism, the American way of life, that sort of thing. Think about it. He was working in a space much like this when he decided to embrace communism. The face tattoo was a sort of direct rebellion against the way things work in Western culture. He's not keeping this place to honor anything. He comes here to defile it, just by standing in it."

Kayne had stopped and reached out to pick up a small replica of the Statue of Liberty. She placed it back on the table, and slowly turned in place, shining her flashlight over the cubicles, the walls, the posters and other objects in the room. "All American," she said, marveling. "Every poster, every tchotchke. This place really is an of homage to America."

"Not an homage," Kotler said. "A curse. Jessup sees this as a symbol of everything he hates."

"And so he works tirelessly to keep it in pristine condition," Kayne said, shaking her head.

"We often focus so much on our enemies that we preserve them," Kotler said.

They were both quiet for a moment, but then startled by the return of the sound.

Scraaaaaaaape.

They turned, flashlights aimed in the direction of it. Kotler gripped the gun. Kayne picked up the miniature Statue of Liberty, hefting it like a small mace.

They moved forward.

Kotler was getting a little nervous about their surroundings. It might look like a typical office space, but they shouldn't let themselves be fooled. This was the Comrade's territory. He knew this place better than anyone. That made every door, every cubicle, every dark corner dangerous.

They moved deeper until they came to a veritable maze of stacked office supplies and books. Everywhere they looked there were towers of boxes, filled with reams of paper. And peppered in among these were stacks of paperbacks and hardbacks, piles of the Comrade's spoils from town. Kotler glanced at some of the titles, and knew instantly why they were here, as part of the Comrades curse of the West, rather than neatly shelved in one of the many libraries lining the corridors.

These titles were all pro-American. Books about American history, about the rise and benefits of capitalism, about right-leaning politics. These books—likely never read, though Kotler couldn't be sure—were the soul of the Comrade's curse. The philosophies and ideals of the nation he hated, encapsulated in each tome, stacked in exile from the rest of his library.

Kotler was examining one of the other stacks when Kayne put a hand on his arm. He glanced up, looking in the direction she was staring.

In the midst of the towers of books and copier paper, briefly visible in their flashlight beams, they saw a dark figure.

The Comrade.

He moved quickly, and before they could even shout for him to stop he'd disappeared in the stacks.

"This isn't good," Kayne said. "There's no way to track him in here."

As if this had been his cue, suddenly a stack of boxes containing reams of paper toppled toward them.

As they both leapt aside, in opposite directions, the Comrade stepped out in front of Kotler.

With speed Kotler couldn't have predicted the Comrade raised the hooked blade and swiped it outward.

It was all Kotler could do to dodge, falling back against another tower of printer paper boxes, toppling it and himself into a jumble on the floor.

Kotler's gun went skittering into the darkness, along with his flashlight.

The light, at least, was still visible, shining in Kotler's direction, enough to allow him to see the silhouette of the Comrade as he raised his blade, preparing to strike and end Kotler, right then and there.

Kayne slammed into the Comrade from the side, roaring as she tackled him to the ground. She was on top of him, and had the miniature Statue of Liberty in her hand, raised to strike.

The man moved and rolled, managing to throw her off of him with great force. Kotler watched as she was slammed into a nearby file cabinet. She looked dazed.

The Comrade was getting to his feet, and so was Kotler.

"Hey!" Kotler shouted and then flung a ream of printer paper at the man's head.

It struck, knocking the Comrade backwards. He shouted and raged, reaching to his head and pulling away fingers covered in blood.

The paper had made an effective enough weapon that Kotler tried flinging another, but now the Comrade was ready. He struck the ream down in mid-air with his hooked weapon and then rushed Kotler. The hook raised in the air and then lashed down with lightning speed, catching Kotler in his outer left thigh as he rolled to dodge.

Kotler let out a cry of pain, but pressed his hand to the wound and limped quickly, deeper into the maze of boxes and file cabinets.

The glow of the flashlight was left behind, and now Kotler found himself in mottled darkness, moving as quickly as he could on his injured leg, trying to stay quiet and stay low.

"American pigs!" the Comrade was shouting. "Capitalist scum! You come here, to *my home*, and try to take this place from me? You attack me! I will end you!"

Kotler had managed to move to a far corner of the room, but he heard the commotion of boxes and stacks of books being toppled. The Comrade would tear down his own shrine to rid it of the American scum.

There was another roar, and Kotler recognized Kayne's voice. She must be attacking the Comrade again.

She was brave as hell, but Kotler wasn't sure she was a match for this guy. He was tougher than he looked. Faster than he looked.

Kotler had to do something.

His gun was lost, but what else did he have?

Looking around frantically, he was coming up blank. There were very few usable resources here. Nothing he could use as a weapon.

He took a deep breath, shook his head, and then stepped back out.

If he couldn't find a weapon, he'd just have to be the weapon.

Maybe two against one would be enough.

KAYNE DECIDED SHE WAS NUTS. Because no matter how hard she hit this guy, he just kept coming back at her, twice as hard. And that blade in his hand was like an extension of his arm. He never lost his grip on it. Never dropped it. And it moved like lightning.

He swung it at her head, and she barely ducked in time. But the Comrade wasn't finished.

He may have missed, but he was able to pivot, to raise the blade again, and then to bring it down on the exact spot where Kayne would have been standing, if she hadn't managed to dive and roll.

She met with one of the towers of books, knocking it over. Dozens of paperbacks fell on top of her.

"You'll both be fertilizer by morning," the man said, his voice low and sure.

Kayne was starting to think he was right.

She rolled onto her back, looking up at him in the low light from the flashlights, which were scattered around the room.

That was one disadvantage they had. Low light.

The Comrade knew this place better than they did. He was used to it. They were fumbling around, trying to stay out of his reach, but getting themselves more and more mired in the Comrade's lair.

Something clicked for Alex, and she couldn't believe she hadn't thought of it before.

The Comrade was standing above her, and he raised the blade then brought it down, hard and fast.

She rolled, kicked at his knee, and as he cried out in pain and crouched to keep from falling over, she scrambled to her feet and sprinted into the furthest, darkest corner she could find.

"You can't run!" the Comrade yelled. "You can't hide! You'll be fertilizer by morning!"

"Kayne!" Kotler's voice rang out in the darkness.

"Keep him busy!" Kayne shouted back.

She couldn't see Kotler, but she knew he was injured. She hoped she hadn't just sent him to his death. She wasn't sure she could live with herself.

She wasn't even sure if she'd live long enough to not be able to live with herself.

But she had a plan.

She found a space—one of the cubicles that backed up against the far wall of the office. She ducked inside, and took out her phone, trying to keep the light of the screen hidden.

Using QuIEK, she brought up everything she had on the Pit. She found what she was looking for and started working.

It really came down to telling QuIEK to link to the quantum processing that was apparently still happening in this facility—negotiate with the strange LTE signal and communicate with the system that kept things running here. She'd done this to open the door, but maybe there was more she could do.

QuIEK caught on to what she was trying to accomplish and assisted.

Lights snapped on all around them.

But more than that.

Throughout the facility, a trail of lights was clicking on, pointing the way to where they were.

"Agent Denzel," Kayne said to her phone. "Agents Symon and Mayher... follow the yellow brick road. All lights lead to us, and to our bad guy!"

"Roger that," Denzel's voice came back. "I'm on my way."

"So are we!" Symon said.

Kayne smiled, then slumped, slipping her phone back into her pocket. She looked around, breathing heavily.

The cubical farm was lit up now. She could make out every detail. The light was comforting, in its way, but it was still an eerie feeling, being here in this place knowing what it was and what it was for.

"Turn them off!"

She was startled and looked up to see the Comrade standing only a few feet away. The curved and wicked blade was raised, ready, hungry.

This was it.

"Turn off the lights!" the Comrade shouted, and for the first time Kayne realized that there was a note of fear and panic in his voice.

He was afraid of the light?

No, she thought. *He's afraid of this place. This American, capitalist symbol. He doesn't want to see it in the light.*

She was going to say something, to snap a witty remark his way, maybe. She was going to tell him to go to hell. But before she could say anything, he lunged to kill her.

A sudden scream changed all the Comrade's plans.

Kayne had closed her eyes, waiting for the inevitable. When she opened them, she saw the Comrade standing only a foot or so from her. She saw the arm holding his wicked blade slowly lower, the blade falling to the floor. And then, seconds later, the Comrade joined it there.

Kayne blinked, not quite sure if she could believe what she was seeing.

The Comrade was lying face down and embedded in the back of his skull was some sort of blade. Something sort of familiar, but still unbelievable.

Is that a paper cutter?

"Kotler?" She asked, looking up and past the heap of the body at her feet.

"Wasn't me," Kotler huffed from somewhere beyond the cubicle wall.

Kayne scrambled to her feet, rising slowly, unsure how much she should trust what was happening.

Standing outside of the cubicle, huffing and panting, eyes wide with some emotion—fear or horror, Kayne couldn't be sure—was a woman. A woman Kayne had only seen in photographs.

"Dr. Rivers?" Kayne asked.

Rivers didn't look at her. She just stared at the Comrade, and then at the curved blade.

"Móki," she said quietly. She looked at Kayne, and then back at Kotler, who was limping into the space, leaning on one of the cubicle walls for support. "That's what he called that... thing. 'Móki.'"

"Death," Kotler said, quietly. He looked at Kayne, and she was giving him a strange expression, shaking her head.

"Móki the Hopi word for death," Kotler offered.

Kayne looked down now at the Comrade's lifeless body.

"Death," she repeated, nodding.

She kicked Móki away from the Comrade's dead hand. Just in case.

The three of them were standing in those exact positions when the FBI agents burst into the room. All three had weapons raised and were yelling commands.

The commotion ended quickly once they realized that Kotler, Kayne, and Rivers were all good guys, and all safe.

Kayne stepped over the Comrade's body, out of the cubicle. She went to Dr. Rivers, who was standing as still as a stone, staring at the Comrade. Kayne tentatively reached out, and in an instant Rivers gave over, allowing herself to be enfolded in a hug, sobbing into Kayne's shoulder. It seemed like exhaustion more than anything. Relief. She didn't seem injured, but there were signs she might be in shock.

Kayne gently directed Rivers to another part of the office, finding a chair for her to sit in. She stayed with her as the agents checked on the Comrade and started making calls to the outside—facilitated by QuIEK, and relaying from Kotler's iPad.

It was over.

The mission was complete. Kayne was seeing the aftermath. She knew what that meant.

Rivers had been rescued.

The day had been saved.

The agents were on the scene.

Now, it was time for Kayne to go to prison.

CHAPTER FOURTEEN

KOTLER WAS STANDING beside their 4x4. His leg had been bandaged, and he'd been given pain killers. He was, by most rights, feeling pretty good.

Denzel was standing with Agents Symon and Mayher, the three of them debriefing. They'd already gotten statements from Kotler, Kayne, and Rivers.

Dr. Rivers herself was sitting in the back seat of the 4x4 that Agent Symon had brought in. Agent Barr's body was still inside the Pit, covered, and waiting for the team of agents, paramedics, and other personnel to arrive.

Alex Kayne was handcuffed to the front of Symon's vehicle.

It wasn't right.

They wouldn't be here, without her. Kotler, at least, would be dead twice over. They'd likely have spent days trying to get into the Pit without her, and in that time Dr. Rivers would likely be dead as well.

Alex Kayne had saved the day. One out of many times she'd

done so, at great personal risk. At the risk of both life and liberty.

It wasn't right, that she was shackled and waiting to go rot in a cell somewhere, buried, her only hope of freedom coming the cost of giving the government a weapon too powerful for anyone to control.

Anyone other than Alex Kayne.

Kotler moved to her, limping, but determined. He leaned against the front end of the 4x4 and shook his head.

"I'm sorry," he said.

"For what?" Kayne asked, giving him a wisp of a smile.

"For getting you into this. For getting you arrested."

Kayne shrugged. "It happens. I knew what I was getting into. I've been in positions like this before."

Kotler nodded. "So what happens now?"

Kayne shook her head. "No way to know, honestly. But best-case scenario is they put me into a deep, dark cell somewhere and keep me there until I agree to give them QuIEK."

"And... will you?" Kotler asked, eyeing her.

She smiled. "Doesn't seem likely."

Kotler shook his head. "So you'd rather sit in prison for the rest of your life than trust the US government with this tech?"

She sighed. "Is it just the US government? When this started, it was the Russians, and the US government, and who knew who else. QuIEK—it isn't just a piece of software, you know. It's the ultimate digital skeleton key. And it's also an advanced AI. You can tell it what you want, and it can go make it happen. Like a genie. It's better if someone smart is at the helm, but it's dangerous enough all on its own."

Kotler considered this and nodded. "When you made it, I'm sure that the intention was something good, right?"

"It was," she said, looking off toward the hillside, her eyes soft. "I was stupid enough to think it would make the world a better, safer place."

Kotler thought for a moment, then said, "I think that's exactly what it's doing. Of course, with someone smart at the helm."

She looked at him then nodded, laughing lightly.

Kotler sighed. "Well, maybe I can put in a good word? And so can Denzel and Symon. I'm sure Liz—Director Ludlum—could do the same. It might help."

Kayne was watching him and shrugged. "It might. Thank you."

He sighed. "It's the least I can do, since you saved my life in there."

She laughed. "I think we both owe Dr. Rivers for that one," she looked back to see Clara Rivers sleeping in the back seat. "She's the brave one."

"Yes," Kotler agreed. "Plenty of brave ones here, though. And you're one of them."

Kayne shrugged again.

It was at that moment that a sound started echoing over the hills. The chop-chop-chop of a helicopter.

"They got here faster than I expected," Kotler said, shifting to get a better view of the approaching chopper.

"Yeah," Kayne agreed. But there was something in her voice that made Kotler look at her.

She was standing beside him, as before. But her hands were free.

She held up a small piece of flat metal, about the width of a fingernail, maybe six inches long. "Hold this for me?" She handed him the little shim.

Kotler's eyes were wide, and a smirk slowly appeared on his face. "You did tell us you were going to get a helicopter," he said.

She smiled at him, then turned and sprinted down the hillside, toward the approaching aircraft.

"Hey!" Denzel shouted, and he and the other two agents raced forward. "Kotler, did you let her loose?"

"Wasn't me," he said, shaking his head. "I don't have a key."

They ran past him, and he watched as Kayne leapt to clutch a roper ladder that was dangling from the helicopter. The chopper rose then, banking as Kayne held on for dear life, and in moments it disappeared over the hillside, the sound fading as she raced away into the distance.

Kotler looked down at the little shim, then to the ground in front of the 4x4's bumper. He spotted something shiny at his feet and stooped to pick it up.

A ring. And inside of it, a little channel where the metal shim would have fit, disguising it.

He remembered Kayne had been wearing this ring. He'd thought nothing of it, had barely taken note of it.

As the agents stood scanning the skies, Denzel on his phone and giving orders to find that helicopter, to track it and relay back to him, Kotler took a moment to work the shim back into the ring's inner channel. With that work done, he slipped the ring itself into his pocket.

He'd keep it, as a little souvenir.

The agents all returned to grill him, and he told them the truth. Kayne had gotten out of the cuffs and had run for the helicopter. He indicated his injured leg, saying that he couldn't have pursued.

Denzel gave him a look, but shook his head.

Soon enough, their own helicopters arrived, and everyone got busy.

He suspected that Denzel and Symon were merely putting on a show of being upset over Kayne's escape. But he knew Denzel well enough to know that he'd been serious about taking Kayne in. Symon, too, seemed the type. They were both duty bound, even if they didn't like the duty.

They had more in common than either man might have thought. It was a shame there was still some animosity between them.

Kotler would have to give a full debriefing later, he knew. But everything was going to be fine.

Alex Kayne, once again in the wind. She wasn't the big story here anymore, if she ever really was.

Things were wrapping up, and Kotler was angling to try to catch a ride home on one of the helicopters, when the real chaos started.

The Pit started to make noise. An alarm sounded, loud and obnoxious, and as all the agents present pulled back, something started happening deep within the mountain. When the noise stopped, a team cautiously entered, and emerged moments later to inform them that many of the tunnels leading into the facility had collapsed.

"They apparently had some kind of security measure in place," one of the agents reported. "Like a self destruct. Charges were set to collapse all the entrances."

"And it just happened to engage after all these years, after we were cleared out?" Symon asked.

The agent had offered some theories, but Kotler had a one already in mind.

Kayne had recognized the danger of what the Pit represented. The quantum encryption and other technology still present in this place might be old school, but it was still dangerous. In the same way QuIEK was dangerous.

And she'd used QuIEK to make sure none of the secrets of the Pit fell into the wrong hands.

It might not be enough. The tech here was likely cataloged somewhere. It was old, by decades, so there was every possibility that some updated and current version of it was in play elsewhere. But as a measure, taking out the Pit wasn't a bad idea.

Kotler glanced toward the horizon, where Kayne had literally ridden off into the sunset.

Some heros get the whole world against them, Kotler thought, smiling. *And they do the right thing anyway.*

EPILOGUE

Kayne sat in a coffee shop in Cypress Park, Texas, about 45 minutes from Austin. She'd been here for the past three days, working out the details of her next case. The events of the past couple of weeks were still fresh, but fading. Just another day at the office.

That was what she kept telling herself.

Her current case involved a lot less "secret government facility" and a little more "overzealous HOA." A master-plan community being a little too quick with the foreclosures was hardly the same as an abandoned secret base full of dark science, but the people who might suffer were just as important, and needed help just as much.

She was working out the best approach to making things right for the homeowners here when she got a chirp from her laptop.

She smiled.

She knew he'd try it. He was just the type.

She opened the browser tab, then looked around at her surroundings, making sure no one could see over her shoulder.

She normally liked to take as many precautions as possible, keep the visual and audible clues to her whereabouts as down low as they could go. But she felt like she was safe on this one. She felt she could trust him.

Which didn't necessarily mean she'd taken *no* precautions.

She'd had QuIEK arrange it so that only Dr. Kotler could use the video chat URL—the same one she'd given him before. If anyone else was present, physically or virtually, or if anyone else attempted to use that link, it wouldn't work.

So it was Kotler, or nothing.

She opened the window and popped in her earbuds.

"Well," Kotler said from her screen. "I didn't think this would work."

"Don't get used to it," she smiled back at him. "It's a onetime thing."

Kotler held up a tiny circle of metal. The ring she'd left behind. "You dropped this."

"Keep it," she said. "Maybe you can return it to me next time we meet."

"So there will be a next time?" Kotler replied.

Kayne smiled. Kotler was a charmer. He was good at getting people to trust him, mostly because he was worthy of their trust. "There always seems to be a next time," Kayne said.

Kotler nodded at this. "How can I reach you? If I ever need to?"

She thought about this. "You still have the same phone? The one you were using at the Pitt?"

Kotler held it up.

"Don't lose it," she said.

"I'll keep it safe," he replied, nodding. "Might get a new one and put this one someplace special."

"Probably a smart idea," Kayne agreed.

"And what about you?" Kotler said, suddenly becoming serious. "Are you... safe?"

"As much as I ever am," she replied. "But thanks for asking."

He nodded again. "Ok," he said. "I just wanted to say thank you for your help. I know what it meant, to put yourself in that position. But I don't think we'd have found Dr. Rivers without you. Oh! She wanted me to pass on a thank you as well, if I ever saw you. So, double thank you."

"And you're both welcome," Kayne smiled. "Now, I have to go. I've got windmills to stab."

"Don Quixote reference? Careful... you don't seem to have a Sancho Panza. And Don Quixote was kind of nuts."

Kayne smiled, laughing lightly. "Fair enough."

Kotler again nodded, then reached out and tapped something on his side. The call ended.

Kayne closed the window. That URL would never work again. But she'd make sure that regardless of what phone Kotler used, there'd be a way to reach her. He just didn't necessarily have to know about it.

She might not have a Sancho, but that didn't mean she couldn't have a friend or two.

It was still true that friends were a luxury she might not be able to afford. But she had a feeling about Dr. Dan Kotler. He seemed to be as much trouble as she was.

And trouble was always best when it stuck together.

A NOTE AT THE END

Most of my books have some kind of quirky origin story. Usually it's tied to some random bit of research I've done, some fact or trivia I've stumbled upon. A few, such as *The Coelho Medallion* and *The Atlantis Riddle* came into being as in-jokes, word play, that sort of thing. Serious books for serious readers, but the behind-the-scenes is quirky.

This book came around because I was invited to participate in a box set with several other thriller authors. *Her Silent Shadow* released around the end of 2020, and mine was but one of around a dozen books to be included.

The theme of *Her Silent Shadow* was "suspense thriller."

I'll confess, most of my books do not fit with this theme. In fact, I bill my Kotler books as "archaeological thrillers," and my Alex Kayne books as "espionage thrillers." If you're looking for those as official ISBN categories somewhere, I'll save you the trouble. They don't exist. They're convenient as labels because readers sometimes go looking for books in those buckets, but that's about as official as it gets.

Suspense thrillers, on the other hand, are a thing in the

ISBN world. That's an "official category." Which you would think would make things somewhat cut and dry... but not so.

Turns out, even though the category is "official," it's a little muddy. It can include all manner of stories, frankly—many of them supernatural in origin (Dean Koontz is considered a suspense writer, as is Stephen King). Some, a very large portion I believe, are what I'd call "psychological thrillers," wherein the protagonist is being terrorized by some force, or forces beyond their control.

So you can see that suspense can lean toward horror. Slasher stories—think *Friday the 13th*—are considered "suspense."

But there's a further complication. Most thrillers, and I'd even argue *all* thrillers, have at least *some* form of *suspense* built into their plots. After all, the term means "a state of feeling excited or anxious, unsure about what will happen." That's kind of Thriller 101, right? It's just good storytelling.

But just like in a court of law, when it comes to books there's the literal truth and then there's the spirit of truth. And that meant I had to face a fact: If I wrote something that didn't fit with the more general notion of "suspense," I was going to use the expectations of the other authors, and more importantly those of the readers.

I needed a more traditional suspense story.

The problem is, as a writer I long ago made the decision to keep copious amounts of sex, violence, and profanity out of my work. Sure, things slip in from time to time. It's hard to tell an action story with no blood, for example. And the hero yelling "Willickers! Gosh Darn!" after being shot is honestly just not appropriate. So I nudge the line of my own principles a little, from time to time. Rules are made to be broken. With tact.

So how was I to write a traditional suspense story without

the requisite copious amounts of sex, violence, and/or vulgarity?

That was problem number one.

Problem number two was more... promotional.

I have multiple series brewing right now, but the two primary series I'm pushing are *Dan Kotler* and *Quake Runner: Alex Kayne*. All my production and marketing energy is going into those series, so I need books that tie in, not distract from. And if I do add new books, I need to somehow connect them to those two series. It's not a granite-hard rule, but I felt strongly that I needed to keep to it.

So there I was with a challenge. I needed to write a traditional suspense story that wasn't going to cause any pearl clutching, but could still enthrall readers. And it had to include at least one of my mainstay characters.

That's when I struck what I think was an elegant solution.

In both of those mainstay series, I've introduced the concept of Historic Crimes—a cross-agency joint operation that includes law enforcement, military, government, and civilian operatives. Kotler is one of those, as a civilian consultant. Kayne is too, as a fugitive with "confidential informant" status.

The two of them were, at that point, completely independent of each other. Or rather, directly independent. To that point, there'd been some bits of crossover as I included Director Liz Ludlum and the whole Historic Crimes task force. Ludlum was the link between the two, then. But the protagonists, and even the supporting characters, had not yet met (though they did reference each other from time to time).

So, here I found myself with an opportunity.

What if I wrote the first crossover between these two series? What if... dare I say it? What *if* both protagonists met and had a chance to work with each other?

And what if they had to face off against a deadly serial killer with a mad agenda?

It was an idea ripped straight from comic books, in my opinion. Like Captain America and Black Widow teaming up for an adventure. Two heroes, one villain, now waiting.

I loved the idea immediately. It served every purpose I had for doing one of these box sets—introducing the characters of my series to new readers, and hopefully encouraging them to go discover the rest of my books. Win-win-and hopefully win!

Did it fit? Was it in the same vein as the stories that would appear in the rest of the box set?

I felt like it could be, if I handled the material right. I was a little concerned that it might be "softer" than the other stories. But I think I rounded it off with the right amount of violence and suspense, by the end. You'll have to tell me.

But from a greater vantage point, what I've done here is essentially create another new series—one that includes crossovers with the heroes and villains of my ongoing stand-alone series. I've opened a door for more adventures like this one, suspense or otherwise.

Historic Crimes is just starting to build steam, in both series, and I've started looking at how to incorporate the rest of my books into this, a budding and growing universe. I think the start of that is this book, along with the intention of many more *Historic Crimes* crossovers to come.

If you enjoyed this, please let me know in a review of the book. You can also email me at kevintumlinsonauthor@ gmail.com.

Also, please do me the honor of recommending this and my other books to your friends and family, anyone who likes a good thriller novel. Tell them they can get a *free* ebook at KevinTum linson.com/joinme. (You can, too).

There will be more crossover events in the future. I enjoyed writing this too much to avoid it. And the Historic Crimes universe will continue to grow and be enriched, to achieve greater depth as more more series are added to that fold. So be on the lookout for all of that, and feel free to write to me and let me know your thoughts.

Until then, thank you for taking the time to read this book.

God bless,
Kevin Tumlinson
Sugar Land, Texas
May 11, 2021

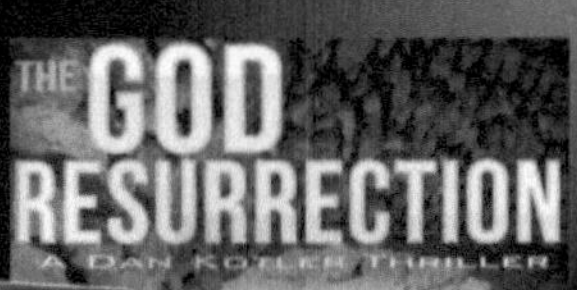

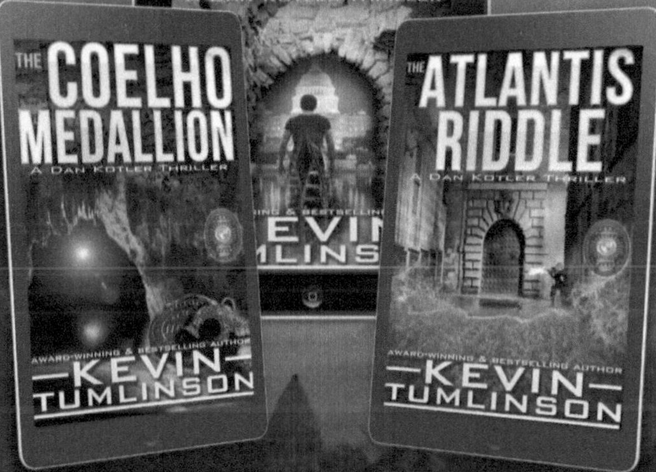

THE THRILLING ADVENTURE AWAITS YOU
DANKOTLER.COM

HERE'S HOW TO HELP ME REACH MORE READERS

If you loved this book, you can help me reach more readers with just a few easy acts of kindness.

(1) REVIEW THIS BOOK

Leaving a review for this book is a great way to help other readers find it. Just go to the site where you bought the book, search for the title, and leave a review. It really helps, and I really appreciate it.

(2) SUBSCRIBE TO MY EMAIL LIST

I regularly write a special email to the people on my list, just keeping everyone up to date on what I'm working on. When I announce new book releases, giveaways, or anything else, the people on my list hear about it first. Sometimes, there are special deals I'll *only* give to my list, so it's worth being a part of the crowd.

Join the conversation and get a free ebook, just for signing up! Visit https://www.kevintumlinson.com/joinme.

(3) TELL YOUR FRIENDS

Word of mouth is still the best marketing there is, so I would greatly appreciate it if you'd tell your friends and family about this book, and the others I've written.

You can find a comprehensive list of all of my books at http://kevintumlinson.com/books.

Thanks so much for your help. And thanks for reading.

ABOUT THE AUTHOR

Kevin Tumlinson is an award-winning and bestselling novelist, living in Texas and working in random coffee shops, cafés, and hotel lobbies worldwide. His debut thriller, *The Coelho Medallion*, was a 2016 Shelf Notable Indie award winner. 

Kevin grew up in Wild Peach, Texas, where he was raised by his grandparents and given a healthy respect for story telling. He often found himself in trouble in school for writing stories instead of doing his actual assignments.

Kevin's love for history, archaeology, and science has been a tremendous source of material for his writing, feeding his fiction and giving him just the excuse he needs to read the next article, biography, or research paper.

Connect with Kevin:
kevintumlinson.com
kevin@tumlinson.net

facebook.com/jkevintumlinson

twitter.com/kevintumlinson

instagram.com/kevintumlinson

bookbub.com/authors/kevin-tumlinson

amazon.com/Kevin-Tumlinson/e/B007POXGEG

ALSO BY KEVIN TUMLINSON

Dan Kotler

The Coelho Medallion

The Atlantis Riddle

The Devil's Interval

The Girl in the Mayan Tomb

The Antarctic Forgery

The Stepping Maze

The God Extinction

The Spanish Papers

The Hidden Persuaders

The Sleeper's War

The God Resurrection

The Demon Core

Dan Kotler Short Fiction

The Brass Hall - A Dan Kotler Story

The Jani Sigil - FREE short story from BookHip.com/DBXDHP

Dan Kotler Box Sets

The Book of Lost Things: Dan Kotler, Books 1-3

The Book of Betrayals: Dan Kotler, Books 4-6

The Book of Gods and Kings: Dan Kotler, Books 7-9

Quake Runner: Alex Kayne

Shaken

Triggered

Compromised

Historic Crimes Crossovers

The Man Below

Evergreen

Evergreen: Book 1
Evergreen: Trace Contact

Citadel

Citadel: First Colony
Citadel: Paths in Darkness
Citadel: Children of Light
Citadel: The Value of War
Colony Girl: A Citadel Universe Story

Sawyer Jackson

Sawyer Jackson and the Long Land
Sawyer Jackson and the Shadow Strait

Sawyer Jackson and the White Room

Think Tank

Karner Blue

Zero Tolerance

Nomad

The Lucid — Co-authored with Nick Thacker

Episode 1

Episode 2

Episode 3

Shorts & Novellas

Getting Gone

Teresa's Monster

The Three Reasons to Avoid Being Punched in the Face

Tin Man

Two Blocks East

Edge

Zero

Collections & Anthologies

Citadel: Omnibus

Uncanny Divide — With Nick Thacker & Will Flora

Light Years — The Complete Science Fiction Library

Dead of Winter: A Christmas Anthology — With Nick Thacker, Jim Heskett, David Berens, M.P. MacDougall, R.A. McGee, Dusty Sharp & Steven Moore

YA & Middle Grade

Secret of the Diamond Sword — An Alex Kotler Mystery

Wordslinger (Non-Fiction)

30-Day Author: Develop a Daily Writing Habit and Write Your Book In 30 Days (Or Less)

Watch for more at kevintumlinson.com/books

KEEP THE ADVENTURE GOING!

GET MORE THRILLS FROM AWARD-WINNING AND BESTSELLING AUTHOR, KEVIN TUMLINSON!

★★★★★ "Half way through I was waiting for Harrison Ford to leap out of the pages!"
—Deanne, Review for *The Coelho Medallion*

★★★★★ "Kevin has crashed onto the action-thriller scene

as only an action-thriller author can: with provocative plot lines, unforgettable characters, and enough adrenaline to keep you awake all night."
—Nick Thacker, author of *Mark for Blood*

★★★★★ "Move over Daniel Silva, James Patterson, and Dan Brown."
—Chip Polk, Review for *The Atlantis Riddle*

★★★★★ "Move Over Indiana Jones, there is a New Dr. in Town!"
—Cycletrash, Review for *The Coelho Medallion*

★★★★★ "[Kevin Tumlinson] is what every writer should be—entertaining and thought-provoking."
— Shana Tehan, Press Secretary, U.S. House of Representatives

★★★★★ "I discovered Kevin Tumlinson from The Creative Penn podcast and immediately got his novel, Evergreen. I read it in like 3 seconds. It's the most fast-paced story I've encountered."
—R.D. Holland, Independent Reviewer

★★★★★ "Comparison to Clive Cussler is a natural, though Tumlinson's 'Dan ' is more like Dan Brown's Robert Langdon than Dirk Pitt."
—Amazon Review for *The Coelho Medallion*

FIND YOUR NEXT FAVORITE BOOK AT
KevinTumlinson.com/books